THE WAR
AT HOME

THE WAR
AT HOME

Connie Jordan Green

Margaret K. McElderry Books
NEW YORK

Lines from the hymn "Beautiful River" by Robert Lowry,
originally published by Abingdon Press, appear on page 65.

Margaret K. McElderry Books
Macmillan Publishing Company
866 Third Avenue
New York, NY 10022
Collier Macmillan Canada, Inc.

Composition by Haddon Craftsmen
Allentown, Pennsylvania
Printed and bound by R. R. Donnelley & Sons
Harrisonburg, Virginia
Designed by Barbara A. Fitzsimmons
10 9 8 7 6 5 4 3 2

Library of Congress Cataloging-in-Publication Data
Green, Connie Jordan.
The war at home/Connie Jordan Green.—1st ed.
p.   cm.
Summary: Living in Oak Ridge, Tennessee, where her father is
involved in a secret government project in the final months of World
War II, thirteen-year-old Mattie carries on a constant debate with
her twelve-year-old cousin Virgil about the relative merits of boys
versus girls.
ISBN 0-689-50470-5
[1. Oak Ridge (Tenn.)—Fiction. 2. World War, 1939–1945—United
States—Fiction. 3. Cousins—Fiction. 4. Sex role—Fiction.]
I. Title.
PZ7.G81925War 1989   [Fic]—dc19   88-26663 CIP AC

To my parents,
Ruth and Early Jordan,
and to my sisters,
Kitty and Sue,
who also knew Oak Ridge in the 1940s.

1

❧♪❀♪❀♪❀♪❧

"CAT GOT YOUR TONGUE, VIRGIL?" MATTIE
asked. Then she hated herself for saying the words that
made her sound just like Gran.

But Virgil wasn't paying any attention to her. He
hunched low in the car seat as the armed guard walked
toward them. With World War II raging across the
oceans, the guards checked everyone who came in or
out of the newly built city of Oak Ridge, Tennessee.
Mattie didn't understand what was so important about
the city, but she had learned to live with the fences
surrounding it and with the guards at all the exits. Now
she couldn't help grinning as she thought how wonderful it would be if Virgil had to have a pass and couldn't
get one.

But, of course, that wouldn't happen. Kids came into
Oak Ridge with adults and left with them anytime. It
was only grown-ups who had to wear the numbered
plastic cards with their pictures in order to get in or out
of the city.

The man in the crisp khaki-colored shirt and pants,
pistol buckled at his waist, flicked his eyes from the
badge Daddy held up back to Daddy's face. Then he
bent over and stared into the car. He looked at twelve-

year-old Virgil in the front seat, at thirteen-year-old Mattie as she tried to appear nonchalant in the corner of the backseat, and at the empty seat beside her.

Mattie thought of how scared she'd been last summer when the family had entered Oak Ridge for the first time. The guard had told Daddy to open the trunk of the car. Then Daddy had taken out their suitcases and opened them, one by one. The guard had looked casually at the piles of neatly folded clothes. Then he let them go.

But even though he hadn't messed with their clothes, Mother still didn't like the search.

"Nosey, isn't he," she said, as they drove away.

"Now, Lucy, he's just doing his job."

"I guess his job is to insult innocent people."

"Most of the time they just look at your badge and wave you on. But they have to check about every ninth or tenth car just to keep everybody honest." Daddy reached over and patted Mother on the knee. "It wasn't anything personal."

"Personal or not, I don't like the idea of somebody checking us."

Mattie had leaned forward, eager to hear how Daddy would reassure Mother. Months had passed from the time he had applied for the job until he had been hired. And the neighbors had all told them they'd been questioned about Daddy by FBI agents. She hadn't given much thought to the questioning; however, the sight of Oak Ridge and its tight security made her wonder.

But Daddy was not very comforting. "All I know," he said, "is that whatever is going on has something to do with the war effort. None of us know what we're working on, and we're warned not to say a word about our jobs."

"What was the guard looking for in our suitcases?" Mattie had asked.

Daddy had only shrugged. Ever since, Mattie had wondered what sort of thing she might have innocently brought along that would have caused the guard to keep them from entering Oak Ridge.

Now, as Daddy drove the car away from the gates, Virgil resumed his talking.

Mattie sighed loudly. Her cousin had talked nonstop during the six-hour drive from the mountains of eastern Kentucky to east Tennessee. The crooked roads were enough to make her feel half sick, and keeping all the windows closed against the damp March air hadn't helped. The sound of Virgil's voice had almost finished the job. After the first hour she'd grown tired of turning her head from Daddy to Virgil and back again in order to follow their conversation. She had tucked her feet up on the seat, leaned her back into the corner, and pretended she was on a bus going to a place she'd never seen. Might as well actually be going, she thought. Daddy and Virgil wouldn't have noticed anyway if she'd vanished into thin air.

And here they were taking up where they'd left off a few minutes earlier. As they drove along the Turnpike, the main street in Oak Ridge, toward the west end of town, Virgil wanted to know what each building was, why the people were standing in line, and why the buses and buildings were all the same drab green.

And, of course, Daddy answered the questions in his usual cheerful voice. To listen to him, you'd think

Daddy was glad Virgil was coming to live with them for a while.

Well, Mattie hoped someone was glad. When she was younger, she had liked having Virgil as a playmate. But he had changed during the last year or two. Now he drove her crazy with his talk about how much better boys were at everything than girls. And whenever Daddy was around, Virgil monopolized him.

When Mattie could stand the front-seat conversation no longer, she interrupted.

"I hope Mother has supper ready. I'm starving to death."

Daddy nodded to her. "I don't doubt she'll have fried chicken and mashed potatoes ready for a celebration."

"What celebration?"

"Why, us bringing Virgil down to Tennessee."

Virgil twisted in his seat and grinned at her. Mattie wanted to cross her eyes and stick her tongue out, but she saw Daddy watching her through the rearview mirror. So she turned her face to the window and concentrated on the colorless scene sliding by.

Finally they left the Turnpike, followed Illinois Avenue up a hill, and turned left onto West Outer Drive. Mattie could see the Cumberland Mountains rising to the west. They were gentle mountains, etched in purple against the setting sun or tipped with white against a bright winter sky. They were not like the mountains she'd lived among in Kentucky. There, the valley between the ridges was so narrow there was room only for the dirt road bordering the creek and for the houses with their tiny lawns. Eastern Kentucky mountains were so crowded together that the valleys received direct sunlight only during the midpart of the day.

"Here we are," Daddy said, as he pulled the gray Ford off the gravel road onto the edge of their lawn.

Mattie looked at her home. The land surrounding the house required a great deal of imagination to be considered a lawn. The yard was rocky red clay with oaks stretching overhead thirty feet before they branched out into limbs and leaves. Like the rest of the recently built city, the yard was muddy in the March rains.

"Gol-ol-lee," Virgil said, as the three of them stepped from the car. "What a long house you've got, Uncle Omer."

Daddy laughed. "We'd be in fine shape if we could just live in all of it. Nope, Virgil, this is what the government calls a T.D.U., a Twin Dwelling Unit. Only, everybody who lives in one hopes it's a *Temporary* Dwelling Unit."

"Yeah, real temporary," Mattie muttered. At least for you, Virgil, she wanted to add.

Mother and Janie Mae rushed down the front steps toward them. Mother and Daddy hugged each other. Mother always seemed so happy when Daddy came home, even when he'd only been away at work for the day. And when they'd been apart overnight—well, you'd think they had never expected to see each other again. Mattie smiled to herself. She was glad they acted that way. The rest of her relatives seemed to think they'd break one another's bones if they did more than lightly pat each other on the back.

Virgil stood to one side, grinning as he held his battered suitcase, which was tied shut with a rope.

Six-year-old Janie Mae wrapped her arms around Mattie's waist. Mattie bent over and squeezed Janie Mae. The warm, clean smell of her hair and freshly ironed clothes was like a balm to Mattie's nose after the stuffiness of the car.

"I had the dream again, Mattie," Janie Mae whispered. "And I . . . I . . ." She looked at the ground, her voice so low Mattie could hardly hear her. "I wet the bed again."

Mattie squeezed her tighter. "It's okay, Janie Mae. I'll be here tonight, and you won't have to be scared."

They climbed the steps to the small porch and went into the living room.

"This is where we live, Virgil," Mother said, waving her arm toward the room. "Makes coal-company houses look like the Ritz, doesn't it?"

The kitchen and living room were separated only by a large metal coal stove. A sofa, two upholstered chairs, and the radio cabinet filled the living room. The kitchen table sat half on the linoleum of the kitchen work area and half on the hardwood of the living room floor.

"You'll sleep on the sofa here," Mother told Virgil, "but you can put your things in the girls' room."

Mattie had emptied the bottom drawer in her dresser and, while Virgil unpacked his clothing into the drawer, she sat on the bed watching him. His wrist bones stuck out from his shirt sleeves.

"Uh, Virgil, have you grown much this year?" she asked.

Virgil straightened and puffed out his chest. "Reckon I haven't been measured for a spell. Do you think I look bigger?"

"No, no, but I was just wondering. A lot of the boys in my class are getting tall really fast."

And it was true. Even though she'd always been one of the tallest in her class, some of the boys were catching up. Maybe with a little luck Virgil wouldn't grow so fast. With him just six months younger than she and in the same grade, she'd felt for years that he was breathing down her neck.

He went back to unpacking, his eyes darting about the room while he worked, his red hair standing up in back where his head had rubbed against the car seat.

"I hear Uncle Omer is with the FBI," he said, as he hung a spare shirt in the closet.

Mattie nearly fell off the bed. "You're crazy. Whoever told you such a thing?"

Virgil looked at her coolly, as if he knew more about her father than she did.

"Oh, everybody back home knows about it," he said.

"Well, everybody back home is crazy."

Virgil smiled as he removed the barrel and stock of a gun from his suitcase. Mattie hardly looked at the weapon. Virgil had always had a BB gun; all the boys she knew back in Kentucky had them. She did her best to ignore boys and BBs or men and their guns. Virgil concentrated for a few minutes on reassembling the rifle, then propped it against the back corner of the closet. He closed his empty suitcase and turned back to Mattie. "You might as well admit Uncle Omer is with the FBI. Sonny Jenkins let the cat out of the bag."

"Now I know you're crazy. Believing what Sonny Jenkins says. Ha!"

Sonny Jenkins was the sheriff of Lloyd County, Kentucky, a position Mattie figured he'd been elected to because he always carried a gun anyway, and everybody hoped they would be better off with him defending them instead of gunning for them.

"Yep, Sonny told everybody the FBI came around

and questioned him about Uncle Omer. He said he figured the only way the FBI would care so much about one man was if they planned to make him a secret agent. So I guess that's what Uncle Omer is now."

Mattie slid off the bed, shaking her head and frowning, and went into the kitchen to see if Mother needed help with dinner. Virgil had been in the house about thirty minutes, and already she felt as if this place that had just begun to be familiar to her had become a stopping-off place for crazy cousins. Having Virgil around was going to be every bit as bad as she'd pictured in her darkest imaginings.

2

MOTHER WAS STIRRING POTS ON THE STOVE
when Mattie entered the living room. Even Mother's
small body practically filled up the work space between
the table and the appliances.

"Mrs. Gwen knows to expect Virgil tomorrow," she
said.

Mattie squeezed into the space beside Mother and
snitched a bit of the brown, crunchy coating from a
piece of fried chicken.

"Aw, Mother, why can't he just stay home with
you?"

"Hush, he'll hear you," Mother said, as she jabbed
the masher up and down in the pot of potatoes. Steam
rose around her head, causing ringlets to escape the
ribbon she used to tie back her hair. "You know he has
to go to school. Why, he may be here a month or more,
depending on how Gran gets to feeling."

Mattie opened a drawer and took out a handful of
silver. Actually, it was silverplate, bought about four-
teen years earlier when Mother and Daddy were married. "We had to save and scrape to pay for it, but I
wasn't going to feed my family from odd pieces left
over from all the old sets the relatives had ever owned,"

Mother had told her. A couple of pieces had been lost in the move from Kentucky, and Mattie noticed that some of the silver was beginning to wear away from the knife handles, showing a darker metal beneath the soft, silvery glow.

She laid a fork beside another plate. Five of them now around the small table instead of the four that had fitted so well. "He'll have to go by himself tomorrow. I'm going to be sick."

"Mix up that margarine for me," Mother said, pointing to a plastic bag of white goo lying on the countertop, a spot of bright orange like an eye looking out of the bag.

Mattie pressed her thumb against the orange spot until it slowly began giving up its color to the white mass. Then she squeezed the bag, working the orange coloring through the white until the bag was filled with a delicate yellow color—not delicate enough to look like real butter, creamy with the rich milk of fat cows grazing in tall green grass, but enough like the real thing to fool them into eating their corn bread with the stuff dripping from the hot slices.

"After all," Mother said as she plopped a glob of margarine into the steaming potatoes, "we want Virgil's life to be as normal as possible."

Mattie wanted to ask what would be normal for Virgil's life, but she figured that would sound mean. Virgil's dad, Jesse Davis, had left him and Aunt Opal when Virgil was a baby. Occasionally someone would mention that Jesse had been seen hanging around a neighboring town, doing a few odd jobs to get by, always at the edge of the law but never actually breaking it. As far as Mattie knew, he never tried to see Virgil.

Then, when Virgil was about one and a half, Aunt Opal had left, too—took off for Dayton and a good-paying job, leaving Virgil with Gran and Gramps. That had been eleven years ago, and Aunt Opal still lived in Dayton. She spent some time with Virgil: Christmas and two or three weekends during the year when she'd catch a ride to Kentucky. And she always brought him presents—trucks sometimes when he was little. After she'd go back to Dayton, Virgil would sit on the linoleum floor and run his new truck around the flowers in the pattern. A few weeks later somebody would step on the truck or it would lose a wheel. Then it would be flung into the creek that wound behind Gran's house, and it would rust there along with the tin cans they emptied of peaches or fruit cocktail or of some other store-bought treat.

If Gran's rheumatism got bad, Virgil would come and stay with Mattie and Janie Mae and Mother and Daddy, or else he would go up on Pinetop Mountain to Uncle Herbert's or around to Aunt Ida's on Beaver Creek. But Mattie knew Virgil liked best staying with them, so she hadn't been surprised a few weeks earlier when Mother got the letter saying Gran was having another bad spell and Virgil wanted to come to Tennessee. She wasn't surprised either when Mother wrote to assure Gran that Virgil could stay for as long as he wanted or when Daddy said he'd go get Virgil.

They hadn't asked her what she thought about it. And now here Virgil was, settling into their home as if they were still back in Kentucky among relatives and not off down here in Tennessee, where thousands of strangers crowded the streets and went about their separate lives as if no one else existed.

Everything about life was different here. Mattie liked to ride the buses and imagine about the people who sat around her. She made it a game to pick out the person who looked as if he might have the most interesting life. Then she stared hard, willing her eyes to bore holes in his head so she could read the messages hidden there.

Once a man sitting across the aisle from her looked up as she concentrated on his skull.

"Little lady," he asked, his eyebrows arching high into his forehead, "are you sick?" He rolled the *R* like a river gurgling through a canyon, and he hissed the *S* ominously.

Mattie had nodded her head slowly and leaned back against the seat, hoping she looked pale. Every time she glanced toward him, he was looking at her, his hands on his knees as if he were ready to grab her if she fell off the seat. She closed her eyes, deciding he was a spy who knew she was onto him.

A few minutes later when he climbed off the bus, she was disappointed to see a lunch pail in his hand, the same heavy shoes on his feet as Daddy and the other men on the street wore.

"Mattie!" Mother interrupted her daydreaming. "Quit woolgathering and give me a hand getting this supper on the table."

Mattie sighed as she set the bowl of potatoes and platter of chicken—Daddy had been right about what Mother was cooking—on the scrubbed white enamel of the kitchen table. Home was so ordinary.

But she was used to it, and she even liked the cozy

feel of the house on winter nights. That is, she'd liked it until today. Now, with Virgil in the house, everything felt different.

"Maybe he'll hate school. Maybe he won't make any friends, and he'll want to go back to Kentucky," she said.

Mother's eyebrows arched like those of the man on the bus.

"Well, I guess it's up to us to see that doesn't happen," she said. "After all, he is Family."

Mattie could hear capitals in that final word. Family was a capital-letter word for all her relatives. The people she'd lived among in Kentucky put bloodlines first. They might not hug much, but they took care of those related to them—no matter how much they themselves had to give up.

That night, when Mattie slipped into bed, she snuggled close to Janie Mae, who was already asleep. With the living room coal stove as the only source of heat, the warmth of her sister's body felt good, and Mattie drifted into a deep sleep, free of the twisting mountain roads she'd followed most of the day.

Several hours later she was awakened by Janie Mae's kicking legs and low moans. "Get away, get away," her sister pleaded.

Mattie touched her arm gently. "Wake up, Janie Mae." She continued to whisper to her sister until Janie Mae's legs stopped thrashing.

Janie Mae slowly opened her eyes. She gripped Mattie's arm. "They were trying to catch me, and I couldn't run," she said.

Mattie patted her arm. "It's okay. It was just your dream again."

"But they're always about to catch me, and my legs won't run." Janie Mae shuddered. "And the men just keep getting out of the airplanes. And their eyes are so big."

"It isn't real, Janie Mae. It's only a dream. The war is on the other side of the world." Mattie turned Janie Mae onto her stomach, then she began gently rubbing her sister's back. After a few minutes she felt Janie Mae relax, and she heard the even breathing that told her the nightmare had gone for one more night.

But sleep didn't return as easily to Mattie. She understood Janie Mae's terror. Each time they went to the movies, the war was on the newsreel. The pictures of the Japanese pilots were the worst—pilots with cloth helmets buckled under their chins and goggles pulled tightly around their eyes. When light hit the goggles, the men appeared to have no eyes, just large staring holes where eyes should have been. Mattie knew about Janie Mae's terror. She always looked away from the newsreel, down into her lap where her hands tugged at the handkerchief Mother made her carry. But looking away didn't erase the faces from her mind.

The newsreels fed Mattie's fear also, the fear that had grown in her for more than three years now, since that Sunday in December when they'd all huddled around the radio listening as someone shouted again and again, "Pearl Harbor has been bombed. We repeat, the Japs have bombed Pearl Harbor."

Mattie had no idea where or what Pearl Harbor was, and Mother and Daddy weren't certain. But during the next few days they all learned that the naval base on the Hawaiian island of Oahu was home to many U.S. battleships, which had been destroyed or disabled by the bombing. Even worse, more than two thousand American men had been killed in the surprise attack.

Until that Sunday afternoon Mattie had never heard of a "Jap," either. Mother had explained that "Jap" was a short name for the Japanese people. But Mattie had figured out since that it was more than a short name. People didn't say Jap when they spoke of the history of Japan or of the art and beautiful fabrics produced by the Japanese people. They said Jap only when they talked about the war, so Mattie knew Japs were different from regular Japanese, the ones who wore long flowing gowns of silk and who drew rows of intricate letters on delicate paper.

Mattie finally drifted to sleep, her dreams filled with blank-eyed Japanese pilots stalking aristocratic old men whose beards hung waist-length from their chins.

Next morning Virgil, already dressed, stuck his head around Mattie's doorway.

"Girls sure are lazy," he said. "Uncle Omer's done gone to work and me and Aunt Lucy've got breakfast all cooked." He grinned at Mattie. "Don't you know we've got to get to school?"

Mattie pulled the pillow over her head. Even her dream-filled sleep was better than waking to Virgil. She just knew this was going to be the longest day of her life.

3

IT WAS STILL DARK WHEN MATTIE AND JANIE Mae and Virgil climbed onto the drab green bus at the end of their street. Oak Ridge had no school buses, but city buses ran every fifteen minutes to carry workers to their jobs and young people to their classes.

Mattie was used to being up early. She and Janie Mae had been on the first shift at school since Christmas. They stayed until noon, then another group of students took their place for the afternoon. She had adjusted to going to school in shifts, but she didn't think she'd ever adjust to having Virgil tag along.

Virgil sat next to a window, Janie Mae beside him. Mattie squeezed in next to the aisle.

"Gol-ol-lee," Virgil said as he wiped the foggy window with his coat sleeve. "Ever place you look there's houses and more houses."

Mattie nodded. "And there are people and more people to fill up those houses," she said. "Thousands and thousands of them. More people than I could even imagine when we lived in Kentucky."

It was true. Whole neighborhoods were built overnight. Large sections of houses were trucked in. Then the parts were fastened together and placed on pole supports. Flattops they were called. Some people laughingly called them cracker boxes. But everybody was glad to get one. The houses came ready to move into—curtains hanging at the windows, cupboards and cabinets built into the tiny rooms.

But even such a fast method of building couldn't keep up with the demand, and house trailers stood side by side along the flat part of the valley that had been fenced in to make Oak Ridge.

And there were dormitories—two-story wood-frame buildings where workers who couldn't get housing stayed.

Every time Mother, trying to clean house, cracked her shin on the living room table and complained about their cramped quarters, Daddy reminded her how lucky they were.

"If the waiting list for housing hadn't been pretty short last summer, you and the girls would still be living back home and I'd be batching it in a dorm room."

Mother always stopped fussing when he said that.

Virgil had about worn his neck out looking around by the time the bus lurched to a stop in front of the school. Boys and girls scrambled off and filed into the building. He followed Mattie down the hall to their classroom. She hung her coat on a hook and stashed her mid-morning snack in the cubicle below. He hung his coat beside hers and put his paper sack in the same cubicle.

She slid into her usual seat at a table near the back of the room. He sat beside her.

"Just girls at this table," she told him.

Virgil grinned and moved to another table, where

Tom Mullins made room for him. Mattie noticed that the boys at Eddie Carmichael's table were nudging each other and pointing at Virgil. She frowned. Even if he was a thorn in her flesh, she didn't want Eddie and his crew to start in on Virgil.

As the bell rang, Mrs. Gwen came into the room. She pulled out her roll book and scanned the names. With so many families moving into Oak Ridge, it wasn't unusual to have new students every few days.

She went down the roll, calling names and putting a check by those who answered.

"Virgil Davis," she said.

There was no response.

Mattie looked at Virgil. He sat at the table, looking as if he were thinking hard about something. What was the matter with him? Had he gone deaf?

Mrs. Gwen glanced around. "Virgil Davis," she said again.

This time Virgil spoke. "That's not my name, ma'am."

Mattie's jaw dropped. Virgil wasn't deaf—he was crazy.

Mrs. Gwen turned to her, a puzzled look on her face. "I don't understand, Mattie. Your mother said your cousin would be coming with you today. But this isn't he?"

"This is Virgil," Mattie said.

"Yes, ma'am," Virgil said, "I'm Mattie's cousin. But I don't go by the name of Davis."

Mrs. Gwen picked up her pencil. "I see. Then what name shall I put on my roll?"

Virgil scratched his head. "Well, mostly I go by my

granny's name because I stay with her most of the time. That'd be Turner. But I'll be staying a while with Mattie here, so you can put down McDowell if you want to."

Mattie bent to her book, hoping the hair hanging over her face would hide her red cheeks. She felt as if everyone were looking at her. Well, did they think she was responsible for whatever Virgil did? She couldn't help it if he enjoyed calling attention to himself. Yes, having Virgil at school was going to be every bit as bad as she'd thought it would be.

However, after roll call, the morning went surprisingly well. Virgil hung around with Tom and his buddies and hardly paid any attention to Mattie. She did her best to pretend that this day was just like any other and that the new boy in class had nothing to do with her. She sat with her friends in the cafeteria when they had their mid-morning break, and she and another girl turned the jump rope for the young ones when the classes went out for a recess.

At the beginning of the recess period, Virgil lounged against a tree, watching Mattie and the rope jumpers. When Eddie walked over to him, Mattie was close enough to hear their conversation.

"Where'd you say you're from?" Eddie asked.

"Kentucky," Virgil answered with a smile. "Ever been there? It's pretty country, mountains and . . ."

"Naw. I've never been there. They don't grow boys very big up there, do they?"

"Not too big," Virgil said, still smiling. "But they grow them tough."

"How tough?" Eddie stepped closer to Virgil. "Tough enough to fight me?"

Virgil stopped smiling. "Fight you?"

Just then Mrs. Gwen blew her whistle. As Eddie rejoined his friends, he threw one last taunt at Virgil. "What's the matter? Are you scared to fight?"

Virgil looked at Eddie's retreating back, shrugged, and fell into step with Tom as the class went back into the building.

At noon, as Mattie and Virgil stood in front of the school waiting for a bus, Eddie sauntered past. "Hey, Virgil, where'd you get that red hair?" he asked.

Virgil grinned. "Came with my head," he said.

"Yeah, well, maybe you could trade the whole thing in."

Virgil didn't answer, just looked up the street, where a bus was topping the hill.

"Maybe you could find some yellow hair to match that yellow streak of yours," Eddie said.

Mattie saw the muscle tighten along Virgil's jaw. It was a warning all the Turners gave when they were getting mad. She'd learned long ago to stop what she was doing when Mother's jaw tightened.

But Eddie obviously didn't know about the Turner jaw.

" 'Course they might not deliver the yellow hair to the right person. They wouldn't know whether to bring it to Virgil Davis or Virgil Turner or Virgil McDowell."

The boys surrounding Eddie roared with laughter and cuffed him on the shoulder with their fists.

Virgil stuffed his lunch bag into his pocket and dropped his notebook. Fists clenched at his side, he turned toward the group.

Eddie and his friends didn't know about the short Turner fuse either.

One of the boys stepped forward, unbuttoning his jacket.

"I don't have no quarrel with you," Virgil said to him.

Eddie remained in the center of the group.

Virgil stepped closer.

Mattie held her breath. What would Mother say if Virgil got in a fight his first day at school?

Then a bus pulled up to the curb. Eddie and his friends laughed as they turned their backs and swaggered to the open door. "Guess you were lucky this time, Virgil," Eddie called. "But you won't always be."

Virgil stood looking after them, the muscle in his jaw like a ball bearing rolling along the bone. His hazel eyes appeared green, and his hair looked redder than usual.

In spite of her personal feelings about Virgil, Mattie didn't like to see Eddie bullying him this way. She timidly laid a hand on his arm. "Don't pay any attention to Eddie," she said. "He thinks he's tougher than anybody around."

Virgil shrugged off her touch. "He started all this, but I reckon I don't mind finishing it."

"You start fighting at school and Mother'll send you back to Kentucky."

Virgil gazed steadily at her. His eyes had lost their glitter, but his jaw was still set. "I reckon girls and women don't understand fighting."

Mattie felt her own jaw tightening. "All right, Virgil Davis-Turner-Whatever," she said. "You just go right ahead and fight. You or Eddie—one of you is going to get beat up, and I don't much care which."

And then we'll see how long you stay in Oak Ridge, she added silently.

4

❧ ♪❂♪❂♪❂♪❂❦

SATURDAY FINALLY ARRIVED, AFTER WHAT
Mattie felt certain had been the longest week of her
life. Virgil had made friends with everyone in the class
except Eddie and his cronies, who had apparently sin-
gled Virgil out for special persecution. But it didn't look
as if Virgil and Eddie were ever going to actually fight.
Eddie had come out of the school building each day just
in time to get on his bus, flinging taunts toward Virgil
but remaining in the center of his circle of friends as he
passed by. Virgil's jaw grew tighter and tighter each
time he looked at Eddie.

Saturday was Mattie's favorite day of the week.
While she rubbed polishing oil into the radio cabinet,
she listened to *Let's Pretend*. One of her favorite stories
was on, the tale of Bluebeard who wouldn't allow his
wife to go into one room, which he kept locked. Bluebeard's wife was turning the key in the lock when
Virgil, carrying a bucket of coal for the stove, burst in.

"That your last chore, Mattie? I'm all done now, and
I'm going exploring. Wanta come?"

Mattie frowned at him, shook her head, and leaned
closer to the radio.

Just then Janie Mae came in from the bedroom,

where she'd been playing with paper dolls. "Can I go with you, Virgil?" she asked.

"Sure," Virgil said. "You can show me what's in those woods behind the house. Don't you wanta go, too, Mattie?"

Mattie snapped off the radio switch. "I might as well," she said. He'd made her miss her favorite part of the story, the moment when the wife looks into the room and sees the weapons Bluebeard used to kill his other wives. Besides, she didn't think it would be fair for Janie Mae to have to put up with Virgil all by herself.

Mother looked at them from the kitchen table, where she sat writing a letter. "Wear your sweaters," she said. "Remember, it's just barely spring."

They trooped back to the bedroom for their wraps. When Virgil looked in the closet for his jacket, he saw the gun he'd placed in the corner when he arrived. "I just might need you, ole buddy," he said, tucking the gun under his arm.

Mother didn't look up again as they left.

The sun shone warmly, something that didn't happen very often in Oak Ridge, it seemed to Mattie. Puddles still stood in the red clay soil, and Mattie remembered the day last summer when they'd moved into the house. Janie Mae had washed her dolls' clothes in a muddy pool, and the pastel dresses had picked up the color from the red clay so that even now they were antique-looking, like old lace stored for a long time in a trunk.

Mother had been too busy unpacking boxes to get mad at Janie Mae; but later, as she tried to get the stain out of the clothing without using bleach on the delicate fabrics, she had fussed at Janie Mae. "These were dresses you and Mattie wore when you were babies, and now look at them," she said.

Janie Mae's lip quivered at Mother's words, and Mattie put a protective arm around her. "She didn't mean to ruin them. She just thought she'd wash them like we used to in the creek."

Mother looked at Mattie sharply. "I know that, Mattie," she'd said. "But Janie Mae needs to know that what she did had a bad result even if she did it for the right reason. She's old enough to start taking responsibility for herself." Mother held a dress at arm's length and shook her head. "You're going to have to start letting your sister develop a tougher hide."

But Mattie couldn't do it. She was the one who slept with Janie Mae, who knew how everything that was said to Janie Mae during the day came out in her dreams at night, how she thrashed her legs and moaned. And how, if Mattie wasn't there to comfort her, her terror grew and grew until finally she wet the bed, waking herself. Mother knew about the dreams and the bed-wetting, and she attempted to reassure Janie Mae whenever she heard her at night. But usually it was Mattie who calmed her sister. And she intended to protect her from whatever frightened her.

However, Janie Mae's night terrors and the war and the other hurts that brought them on seemed far away to Mattie as she stretched her arms in the warm sunlight. Maybe she could even put up with Virgil on such a day. At the edge of the woods, she took off her sweater and hung it on a limb. Virgil and Janie Mae did the same. Then Virgil shouldered his gun again.

Mattie looked scornfully at the weapon. Virgil had

had a BB gun for years. He used to try to get her to shoot it when they were both at Gran's. But Mattie would never touch it. "Guns are a big part of what's wrong with the world today," Mother often said. It was one of the few things about which Mattie agreed completely with her mother.

Mattie took the lead down a steep slope behind the house. "Too steep to build on," Daddy had explained one day, "so the government left it in woods. They call them 'greenbelts' and they're scattered all over Oak Ridge." Mattie was glad she lived next to a greenbelt. Last fall she and Janie Mae had often walked home from school through the woods, the dry leaves crunching beneath their feet.

Today the leaves under her feet were soggy from all the rain. She kicked over a clump of leathery oak leaves, slow to decay, and a rich, moist smell drifted to her nose.

With Janie Mae and Virgil behind her, she headed for the foot of the ridge, where a creek meandered. In nice weather she went there often, jumping from stone to stone until she reached a large rock in the middle of the stream. She liked to sit on the rock and watch the water part and flow past.

But today she heard the water before she saw it.

The three of them gazed upon a muddy torrent roaring down the creek bed and curling around the rock, only the tip of which stuck out of the stream. "Well, I guess I won't sit on my rock today," Mattie said.

"Why not?" Virgil asked.

"Because I can't get to it without getting into that muddy water."

"Sure you can."

"Come on, Virgil. You can't even see the stepping-stones."

"So? Who needs stepping-stones?"

"Since I haven't grown wings yet, I need them."

Virgil looked her up and down. "I guess that's right, seeing as how you're a girl."

Not that again, Mattie thought. "And what does being a girl have to do with it?" she asked wearily.

"Just about everything, I reckon. Boys don't think twice about jumping that far."

"Oh, really?"

"Yeah, really."

"Next I guess you're going to tell me *you* can jump that far."

"That's about the size of it."

Mattie leaned against a tree trunk and folded her arms across her chest. "So, prove it," she said.

Virgil paced up and down along the bank. "Okay, I'll do it. But if I make it without getting wet, you gotta jump, too. Or else admit girls can't do what boys can."

Putting up all week with somebody who was crazy was bad. Having to tolerate him on the weekend was double bad.

"Watch my gun, Janie Mae," Virgil said as he leaned the gun against a sycamore growing along the bank.

Janie Mae looked at the gun, but she didn't go near it. "Mother's gonna be mad if you get muddy," she said.

"Okay. Just in case . . ." And Virgil began stripping out of his clothes. When he was down to his under-shorts, he backed several feet away from the bank. Then he bent over, eyed the tip of the rock, and slowly raised his back end in a racer's stance. The next second his feet were thudding against the soggy earth, his arms swinging in rhythm. He ran half crouched to the water's edge. Then he flung himself into the air.

Mattie couldn't take her eyes off the flying figure. Any second now he was sure to land in the muddy water. But to her surprise, his feet smacked safely on the protruding tip of the rock. She stared at him in disbelief. He really could jump that far.

He looked over his shoulder, his mouth turned up in a triumphant smile. But the next minute he paid for it. His arms flailing wildly, the smile frozen on his face, he slowly tipped backward into the water. When he stood up, water swirled around his thighs, and his undershorts were the color of Janie Mae's doll dresses.

He waded out of the creek and grinned at Mattie. "Okay, let's see how far you can jump now."

"Oh, no you don't," Mattie said. "The deal was I had to jump only if you made it dry. And nobody in his right mind would call you dry."

Virgil looked at muddy rivulets streaming down his legs and across his feet. He laughed. "I reckon I did get a little wet."

Dang, Mattie thought, he even loses with good humor.

He disappeared for a few minutes behind a large oak. Then he emerged wearing his blue jeans, shirt, and shoes. He flung his muddy undershorts over a limb. "They'll be dry enough to put back on when we head home. Reckon Aunt Lucy'll never know the difference."

Mattie looked at the muddy undershorts and remembered Janie Mae's doll clothes. She doubted Mother had gone blind since then.

Virgil picked up his gun, and they continued along the creek bank. Downstream, where a fallen tree bridged the creek, they crossed to the opposite bank. Then they climbed the hillside and stood looking out over Oak Ridge. The Turnpike wound like a river far below them. Beyond it more ridges rose. Mattie explained to Virgil that behind those hills lay the Y-12 plant where Daddy worked.

"You mean, that's FBI headquarters?"

Mattie looked at him scornfully. "I told you Daddy doesn't work for the FBI."

"Well, he sure ain't a coal-mine supervisor like he used to be. So what does he do?"

Mattie was stumped. None of them knew yet what Daddy did. Each time they brought up the subject, he said *he* didn't even know and that he wasn't allowed to talk about it anyway. But Mattie had heard lots of guesses about what was going on in those big buildings beyond another circle of fences and guards. Some people said they were making Roosevelt buttons for the next election, but she figured nobody would go to so much trouble guarding the place if that's all they were doing. No, it had to be something connected with the war. Maybe invisible paint for the airplanes. Or a new kind of gasoline since the old was so hard to get. Mother heard rumors they were making silk stockings, but she said that was just wishful thinking on the part of some women who couldn't get stockings with the war going on.

Virgil was grinning again. "Reckon I've done guessed Uncle Omer's secret."

Some things just weren't worth talking about anymore, Mattie decided.

Later, as they headed back up the ridge toward home,
Virgil once more wearing his undershorts under his
other clothes, they heard a noise in a blackberry bram-
ble. Virgil laid a finger against his lips and slipped the
gun from his shoulder. He aimed the muzzle at the
outer edge of the brambles, cocked the hammer, and
waited. In a few seconds a rabbit darted from the brush.
Virgil squeezed gently on the trigger.

A loud explosion ripped the silence of the woods.
The rabbit flipped backward and lay still.

"Virgil, you killed him," Janie Mae shrieked. She
covered her face with her hands and began to sob.

Mattie put her arms around her sister. "It's okay,
Janie Mae," she said. "Maybe he's just stunned. BBs
don't kill rabbits."

Virgil walked over to the animal and picked it up by
its back legs. It hung limply from his hand. He looked
at Mattie. "What're you talking about? BBs? This here
rabbit is dead as can be. If you knew anything about
guns, you'd know this is a twenty-two."

"A twenty-two!" Mattie exclaimed. "Where'd you
get a real gun?"

"It was Gramps's old gun—his J. Stevens Little Scout,
the one he'd had about thirty years. He said it was nice
and small, just the size for a boy. So he gave it to me
for Christmas."

Now Mattie was mad. "Virgil, bringing a gun into
Oak Ridge is the dumbest thing you've ever done. Do
you want to get us all arrested?"

Virgil just grinned at her. "All I want is rabbit stew
for supper."

He tucked the gun beneath his arm and started up
the hill with the rabbit. Janie Mae was still crying and

Mattie stood with her arm around her shoulder.

"You walk out of these woods carrying that gun and you'll go straight to jail," Mattie called.

Virgil stopped and looked at her. "Quit kidding, Mattie," he said, but the grin on his face was not as sure as it had been.

"You better listen to me, Virgil. You don't know much about Oak Ridge."

"What do you mean, I'll go to jail?"

"Just what I said. It's against the law to shoot a gun in Oak Ridge, or even to have one if it isn't registered."

"Aw, come on. With all these hills and woods, everybody must have guns. Don't Uncle Omer come out here and get you a rabbit or a squirrel for dinner sometimes?"

"No, he doesn't. And neither does anybody else who doesn't want to be arrested."

Now Virgil was frowning. He leaned the gun against a tree and studied the rabbit.

Mattie nodded toward the dead animal. "We'd better get rid of it. Then you can hide your gun again. Maybe nobody heard the shot."

Janie Mae had stopped sobbing, but each time she looked at the dead rabbit, her chin quivered and she swallowed hard. Virgil placed the rabbit in a small hole, then he and Mattie hauled rocks and heaped them on the animal. When they were through, Janie Mae made them wait while she found a long, flat rock. She started dragging it toward the mound they'd built.

"Here, I'll do that," Virgil said as he bent to pick up the rock. "Where do you want it?"

"Right here," she said, pointing to the end of the mound. "It's the tombstone."

"Oh," Virgil said.

"Can you make it stand up?"

"I reckon I can." He propped the flat stone against the mound, then wedged another rock behind it. The tombstone leaned toward the grave, but it remained upright.

Janie Mae smiled for the first time since Virgil had fired the gun. "Now, maybe the rabbit likes that," she said.

Virgil shifted his weight from one foot to the other while Janie Mae inspected the stones one more time. Mattie figured he was regretting ever having seen that rabbit.

Finally, they climbed the hill to the edge of the woods. Virgil looked critically at his gun. "I'll have to clean it later when nobody's around," he said. "Reckon I can get it back in the closet without Aunt Lucy seeing me?"

"Just a minute," Mattie said. She pulled their sweaters from the limb where they'd hung them earlier. "Here, wrap these around the gun."

As they went up the steps to the front door, the aroma of simmering pinto beans greeted them. Virgil sighed. "Rabbit stew sure would've been good." He looked quickly to see if Janie Mae had heard him, but she had already gone into the house. He gazed at the bare yard, the mud puddles, and the half of a house he and Mattie were about to enter. "Oak Ridge sure is a strange place to live," he said.

5

MATTIE WASN'T SURPRISED WHEN SHE WAS
awakened that night by Janie Mae's kicking legs. While
she soothed away Janie Mae's terror, she inwardly
cursed Virgil for giving her sister another vision for her
nightmares. But with part of her brain, she knew Virgil
had done only what seemed normal to him and it
wasn't fair to blame him. Maybe boys and guns belonged together. At least, Virgil seemed to think so.
And maybe he was right about something else, too.
Maybe girls and boys were basically different. At least,
Mattie was sure she would never be able to pull a
trigger and kill a rabbit.

On Monday morning Mother was sorting the laundry as Mattie, Virgil, and Janie Mae left for school. She
stopped suddenly and held up a muddy pair of undershorts.

"Virgil," she said, "have you been doing your own
laundry?"

"No, ma'am. Gran always washed my clothes."

"Gran?" Mother said, disbelief in her voice.

"Yes'm. She just threw my clothes in the tub with
hers and Gramps's."

"Well, I can't imagine." Mother shook her head.

"And she used to be so careful about getting things white. Why, this underwear is so dingy, it looks as if it's been washed in mud."

Mattie, Virgil, and Janie Mae all burst into laughter when they were on the porch, the door safely shut behind them.

"Gran wouldn't much like Aunt Lucy thinking she's a bad housekeeper," Virgil said, as he ran down the steps.

"You were just lucky," Mattie said.

He smiled and then started whistling through his teeth. Mattie wondered if things always went his way so smoothly.

The same warm and sunny weather that caused Mother to tackle the pile of laundry also affected Mrs. Gwen. She announced they would have a longer than usual recess period so that they could play softball. A loud cheer drowned out the rest of her words as the class rushed outdoors to the ball field.

"What's this here game called softball?" Virgil asked.

Eddie was standing nearby. He looked at his friends. "I guess if ole Virgil don't know his own last name, he sure wouldn't know how to play softball."

Virgil whirled around, but everyone's attention turned to Mrs. Gwen as she appointed Robert and Beth team captains.

Then began the ritual to determine who would have first choice of players. Mrs. Gwen stood the bat on end and Beth closed her hand around it halfway up its length. Then Robert put his hand just above Beth's, the heel of his hand resting against her thumb and index finger. Mattie stared at Robert's hand. He always chose her for his partner when they folk-danced, and his

palm was always damp. But now his hand looked powerful above Beth's smaller one.

Beth placed her other hand above Robert's and they
continued hand-over-hand up the length of the bat.

"It's gonna be Beth," someone said.

"Nope, there's more room," someone else said.

And he was right. Robert squeezed his hand just
above Beth's. When Beth removed her hand, Robert
lifted the bat, showing he had control of it.

"Your choice, Robert," Mrs. Gwen said.

Robert looked down at the ground where the toe of
his shoe dug a small hole in the dirt. He cleared his
throat, swallowed, then cleared his throat once more.

"Mattie," he said so quietly that only those standing
nearby heard.

But Virgil heard.

"You must be the best player in the whole class," he
said.

"Nah," Eddie said from the middle of his friends,
"she plays just like a girl. Robert's just sweet on her,
that's all."

Mattie felt the redness creep up her neck and flow
into her cheeks as she lined up behind Robert. Merci-
fully, Beth immediately called Tom's name, and the
rapid choosing of players took the attention away from
Mattie. Virgil was chosen nearly last by Robert, just
before Jimmy, who always struck out, and Sarah,
whom everyone called fatso and who could never beat
the ball to base.

Mattie and Virgil took the field along with the rest
of Robert's team. Although Mattie didn't consider herself a good enough player to have been chosen first, she
liked softball and could usually catch any balls that

came her way. Unlike many of her friends, she didn't think it was boring to stand in the outfield. She enjoyed watching the batter and trying to figure from the angle of the bat just where the ball would land.

Tom was first batter and hit a ball that Mattie knew immediately would be over everyone's head, though she started backpedaling as soon as the bat connected with the ball. The ball landed with a dull thud on the boardwalk near the road, an automatic home run by their ground rules. Beth's team scored four more runs before the third out came and Robert's team could bat.

Robert didn't make Mattie first batter, a favor for which she was thankful since attention had now slipped away from her. As he lined up his batting order, he placed Virgil near last.

Mattie caught Virgil's eye as the first batter stepped up. "Why don't you tell him?" she mouthed.

Virgil shook his head and made a circle with both hands, indicating the size of the softball.

Well, maybe he's right, Mattie thought. There are a lot of differences in the two games.

Robert's team scored several hits, but the third out came before Mattie's turn to bat. She returned to the outfield with the score five to three for Beth's team. With the weaker part of the batting order up, Mattie stayed closer to infield and scooped up several balls bounding along the packed red clay surface. A high ball was hit to Virgil, and he easily caught it for the final out. As he walked in to home plate, he tossed the ball lightly into the air. "Sure is a strange one," he said.

Mattie was second up to bat, behind a runner who was safe because the first baseman missed an easy grounder. Tom, pitching for Beth's team, drew back his right arm, stepped forward, and let the ball roll off the tips of his fingers. Mattie tried to keep her eye on the ball, but it was coming fast, and she realized she wasn't going to hit it a second before it swished past her chest. Her bat finished its useless swing.

"Come on, Mattie, we need some runs," Virgil yelled behind her.

Robert rubbed his palms along his blue jeans.

Tom was ready for another pitch. Mattie felt ready this time, too. She knew now that Tom could throw harder than he did last fall. Gripping the bat, she watched the ball approach home plate, making contact just as her arms were extended in front of her. The ball rose into the air, heading for outfield. Mattie ran as hard as she could. As her toe touched first base, her team shouted for her to go on. She rounded the corner and ran lightly down the baseline, the wind like fingers brushing the hair from her face. From the corner of her eye, she saw Jimmy pick up the ball and throw it toward Tom, so she stayed on second.

Just good luck the ball headed for Jimmy, she thought. Maybe a little bit of Virgil's luckiness had rubbed off on her.

But her team's good fortune seemed to be running out. The next two batters struck out. Then Virgil was up.

"Looks like you're gonna have two runners left on base, Robert," someone called from the outfield.

"Yep, Virgil's up, and he ain't never played this game," Eddie taunted from near Mattie. Mattie looked at him, raised her eyebrows, and smiled. Eddie just didn't know about the Turner blood that throbbed through both her and Virgil's veins.

Virgil was at the plate swinging the bat.

"Want me to pitch you one for practice?" Tom asked.

Virgil grinned. "I think I got the hang of it from watching," he said.

Eddie snickered.

Tom drew back his arm and let the ball fly. Virgil wiggled the bat, stepped forward on his left foot, and let his body go into the swing.

The sound of that crack probably carried all the way to Mother's clothesline, Mattie thought, as she rounded third and headed for home.

Eddie's mouth hung open as Virgil passed him.

"Hey, Virgil," someone shouted, "thought you'd never played this game."

"Never have," Virgil said, planting both feet firmly on home plate. "We've got a game back home something like it. We call it baseball, and I don't reckon there's a boy in Kentucky hasn't played baseball since he was five years old."

Because Virgil's hit was the winning run, no one on Robert's team minded when Sarah was called out at first base.

"Next time I'll know how to pitch to you," Tom said good-naturedly as he clapped Virgil on the back. Robert walked into the school with his hand resting lightly on Virgil's shoulder.

Guess he's forgotten, Mattie thought, that he didn't much want Virgil when he picked his team.

6

IT WAS SEVERAL DAYS LATER BEFORE EDDIE once more taunted Virgil. Mattie figured having Virgil as the sports hero had temporarily put Eddie off. However, the calm couldn't last forever, and one day after school Eddie and his friends were grouped around the door as Virgil and Mattie came out.

"Well, Virge, have you got over being a big man with the bat?" Eddie asked.

Virgil just grinned.

"Guess you got lucky that time up," Eddie continued.

"Reckon this rain'll stop someday and we'll find out," Virgil said. The grin never left his face.

Eddie hooked his thumbs in his belt loops and hitched his pants higher, throwing back his shoulders and puffing out his chest. "Wonder how big a man you are without a bat in your hands," he said.

Virgil looked Eddie over from head to toe. Eddie stood a couple of inches taller than Virgil and was ten pounds or so heavier. But Virgil lifted his chin and looked Eddie in the eye. "I reckon I'm big enough for whatever comes along."

Mattie noticed that Virgil was no longer grinning and

that the muscle along his jaw was working. "Come on,
Virgil," she said. "We've got to get Janie Mae and catch
the bus."

"That's right, Virgil," Eddie said. "If you ain't got a
bat to hide behind, then a girl'll do just fine."

Virgil's face went pale, making his red hair blaze, the
way it had that first day when Eddie had harassed him.
His eyes were like green metal as he stepped toward the
group of boys. This time none of Eddie's friends came
forward, fists ready. Instead they fell back, leaving
Eddie facing Virgil.

Eddie rocked confidently on the balls of his feet, but
Mattie noticed he cut his eyes right and left, like an
animal looking for an escape route. Then the roar of a
bus topping the hill filled the silence surrounding them.
Eddie removed his thumbs from his belt loops and
patted back his hair. "Guess you've been saved again,
Virgil. I got to get on my bus now." And he and his
friends walked to the edge of the street, swaggering as
they passed the crowd gathered near.

Virgil clenched and unclenched his fists. "I'll get that
loudmouth yet," he said.

"Aw, Virgil, I've told you he's not worth bothering
about. He just likes bullying people," said Mattie.

"Well, he ain't going to bully me no more."

Mattie shrugged her shoulders. "Suit yourself," she
said. Then she went to find Janie Mae.

She forgot about Eddie until that evening at supper.

"Uncle Omer," Virgil said, "do you reckon a smaller
guy has much chance against a big guy in a fair fight?"

Daddy stopped chewing and looked thoughtful. "I
guess it all depends on the small guy and the big guy
and who knows how to fight best."

Virgil sighed. "I know how to run and jump and play baseball, and now softball, but I don't reckon I've done a lot of fistfighting."

Mother laid down her fork. "Now what's all this talk about fighting?"

"Aw, it's nothing," Virgil said.

"It must be something or you wouldn't have brought it up."

"Naw."

Mother looked at Mattie. "Tell me what's going on, Mattie. You know I don't hold with fighting, and if anybody thinks he's going to be doing any, I want to know about it."

Mattie pushed the pat of margarine deeper into her mashed potatoes. Why did she have to be responsible for the care and keeping of Virgil? He wanted to fight—let him explain it to Mother.

But Virgil didn't say anything, just went on shoveling green beans into his mouth and looking at Mattie as if she had an interesting story to tell.

"I'm waiting," Mother said, an edge of impatience creeping into her voice.

"Oh, it's just Eddie," Mattie said.

"And who is Eddie?"

"He's a boy in our class, a blowhard if there ever was one."

Daddy had gotten interested in the conversation. "Does that mean he just threatens and never does anything about what he says?"

"Well, no," Mattie admitted. "Eddie likes to bully people, but only as long as whoever he's picking on is smaller than he is. He never messes with Tom or any of the guys his size."

Daddy rubbed his palms together. "What do you know about defending yourself, Virgil?" he asked.

"Omer," Mother said, a note of warning in her voice.

"Now, Lucy, every boy needs to know something about boxing."

"Every *person* needs to know more about getting along with other people," she said.

Daddy pushed away from the table. "When you've finished, Virgil, come outside. There are a few things you and I need to talk about."

Mother didn't say any more, just set her jaw in disapproval and began clearing the table.

Mattie swallowed the last of her dinner. "If you'll help Mother clear the table, I'll wash and dry tonight," she whispered to Janie Mae.

Janie Mae frowned. "Only if you'll take me to the movies Saturday."

"Good grief," Mattie said. "Does everybody want something from me?"

Janie Mae crossed her arms over her chest and stayed rooted to her chair.

"Okay, okay. The movies," Mattie said. If mother will let you go, she added silently. Mother tried to protect Janie Mae by keeping her away from the movies with their newsreels, but Janie Mae cried each time Mattie went, so Mother usually relented and let her go along. "It just isn't possible to close ourselves off from the war," she would say with a shake of her head.

Mattie hurried out before Janie Mae could think of any other demands. As she went down the porch steps, she saw Virgil jumping from one foot to another, like someone standing on a hot rock.

Daddy laughed. "That's not exactly what I meant by

footwork, Virgil. A boxer is something like a dancer—graceful on his feet. What you need is some practice." He looked around at Mattie. "Run and get Janie Mae's jump rope for us."

"Orders, orders," she muttered as she went back up the steps.

But running the errand was worth the effort when she saw the expression on Virgil's face as he held the rope.

"Aw, Uncle Omer," he said, "jumping rope is sissy stuff."

"Joe Louis jumps rope several hours every day, and nobody ever accused him of being a sissy," Daddy said. He instructed Virgil on holding the rope and throwing it lightly over his head while he lifted one foot and then another, just enough to clear the swinging rope.

Mattie settled on the bottom step and leaned back. This was going to repay her for every minute of the weeks of putting up with Virgil. He was about to find something that girls could do a lot better than boys.

Virgil seemed to feel the same way. He stood ramrod straight, an end of rope wrapped around each hand. He looked at Mattie several times as if wishing she would go away. Mattie just settled her back more comfortably against the creosote post.

Finally Virgil swung the rope over his head. His right foot lifted over the passing rope, then his left. The rope swung over his head once more, and again his feet lifted smoothly to clear the rope. He grinned at Mattie as he skipped lightly from foot to foot. Mattie stood up, yawned elaborately, and walked up the steps. She hoped Virgil understood she had lots better things to do than watch boys jump rope. But as she went into the house, she saw that Virgil and Daddy were talking animatedly to one another. Neither had noticed that she had gone.

She let the screen door slam behind her.

That night Mattie was awakened before midnight, but not by Janie Mae's bad dreams. She heard a commotion in the hallway, Mother and Dad whispering as they fumbled for the light string. Then light flooded her bedroom, and she slipped out of bed and went down the hallway behind the adults.

Someone was knocking loudly at the door.

Daddy undid the night latch and swung open the door. "Why, Mrs. MacIntyre, come in," he said.

The woman from up the street stood shivering on the porch. She looked toward Mother and opened and closed her mouth several times before she spoke. Mattie was reminded of a goldfish, but one look at her mother's face removed any such lighthearted thoughts. Mother held on to the back of a chair, her knuckles white. Her eyes never left Mrs. MacIntyre's face.

The MacIntyres were the only family on the street with a telephone, and Mother seemed to know that any calls in the middle of the night could bring only bad news.

"What is it, Nancy?" Mother asked.

"Oh, Lucy, I hate to tell you."

Mother slowly nodded her head as Mrs. MacIntyre stepped closer to her.

"It's your sister, Lucy. It's Opal."

Mother glanced toward Virgil. He rolled over on the sofa and opened his eyes.

"What about Opal?" Mother asked.

"There was an accident. She was hurt. Hurt bad."

The words seemed hard for Mrs. MacIntyre to get out, as if each one had been pulled up from way inside her. Mattie thought again of a fish, one she'd caught two summers before. As it lay in the bucket, its breaths seemed to come from way inside it. Then it had barely attempted to breathe, and soon its gills stopped flapping and it lay still. Mattie had been afraid to touch it, it looked so shiny and perfect.

But Mother wasn't afraid of Mrs. MacIntyre. She reached out to her, as if it were she who needed to be comforted.

"Did they say how bad she's hurt?"

Mrs. MacIntyre's face crumpled. "She's dead," she whispered.

Mattie looked quickly at Virgil. He was wide awake now. He swung his legs over the side of the sofa and pulled on the blue jeans lying beside his bed.

Mrs. MacIntyre straightened her shoulders. "They left a number. I told them you'd call in ten minutes. You'd better come to my house."

Daddy was slipping a jacket over his pajama top. "I'll go, too," he said.

Mother looked worriedly at Virgil. "Maybe one of us had better stay. . . ."

But Virgil waved his hand toward her, and as soon as Mother had put on some clothes, the three adults went out the door. Mattie was left alone with Virgil. He stood gazing blankly at the door, his hands hanging limply at his sides. Mattie swallowed hard and moved a step closer to him. What do you say to someone who has just learned his mother is dead? *I'm sorry* didn't seem enough, and *she was a nice woman* was totally inappropriate. How would she feel if it were Mother who was dead? Mother—who peeled mountains of potatoes and ironed heap after heap of clothes. Mother—who was always in the kitchen when Mattie and Janie Mae came in from school, who sewed buttons on their dresses and gave them advice, some of it good, some of it not so usable, on everything from how to answer a smart aleck to what color socks to wear with a plaid skirt. Suppose she knew she'd never again feel Mother's hand brush her cheek as Mother pulled the covers over her and Janie Mae?

But Virgil had never known many of those things Mattie would have missed about her mother. Opal hadn't been the one to tuck him in, and he'd never come home from school to her. Still, she was his mother, and one look at Virgil's face told Mattie that he was feeling his loss the same as she would. She touched his shoulder lightly. His skin was cool and smooth as if it were a part of him that knew nothing of what he'd just learned. He seemed not to know she was there, and she dropped her hand back to her side.

"I'll make us some hot chocolate," she said.

Virgil walked slowly to the kitchen table and pulled out a chair. He perched on the edge of the seat, as if he expected to have to jump up any minute. Mattie stirred sugar into the powdery cocoa—both scarce ingredients with the war going on—clattering the spoon against the saucepan as she worked. The noises she made were a sort of song, and she moved rhythmically from one step to the next. She began to see why Mother and Gran went to the kitchen when something upset them.

By the time Mother and Daddy came back, the chocolate was simmering on the stove, its smell filling the house as if this were Christmas afternoon. They sat at the table with Virgil, who only blinked in a dazed way. Mother laid a hand on his arm.

"We'll leave for Kentucky first thing in the morning. Uncle Omer already called his shift superintendent, and the MacIntyres loaned us their gas coupons."

Virgil nodded. Then he shook his head hard, as if he had water in his ears. Mattie set a cup of chocolate in front of him, and after one sip, he spoke for the first time since Mrs. MacIntyre had told them about Opal.

"Did they say how she . . . what killed her?"

"It was a car wreck. She was riding home with some-body after her shift at work and . . . another car—a drunk probably—ran a red light. He hit the car Opal was riding in . . . hit it right on the passenger's side." Mother patted Virgil's arm. "It was quick. She probably didn't even know what happened."

Virgil nodded again. "It's just . . . I can't get it straight. She was dead while I was sleeping. And I didn't know anything about it. I was sleeping just like I always do. . . ." His voice trailed off.

Mattie poured the remainder of the chocolate into a cup for herself and sat down. Everything was so still that she could hear the ticking of the clock in her parents' bedroom. The people at the table were like actors in a silent movie as they lifted the cups to their lips, drank soundlessly, and quietly set the cups back on their saucers.

Mattie tried to sort out what she knew about death, but she realized it wasn't much. Death had never touched her closely before—except when her dog had died. She looked around quickly, hoping no one could read her mind. She felt guilty to be thinking about a dog's death when they had just learned about Opal.

And yet the days following Buster's death were the worst days she'd ever gone through. They had had Buster ten years, since he was a puppy and she was a baby. She and her dog had played together long before Janie Mae had been born, and then while Janie Mae was too young to really play. Buster had been Mattie's comfort when she had been unhappy. She could wrap her arms around him and bury her face in his warm side, and the lump in her throat would melt away. Or sometimes it would dissolve in warm tears soaking into Buster's fur.

Then one day he darted in front of a coal truck, and he was gone from her life forever. For a week she cried every day when she came home from school and Buster wasn't there to greet her. For months she couldn't bear to read dog stories or to go to movies that had warm, loving dogs in them.

But as bad as that experience had been, she knew the death of a member of the family was much, much worse. Then why weren't they all crying? Why didn't Virgil cry? Or Mother? If Janie Mae had been hit by a drunk driver, Mattie figured she'd be crying. She'd be howling. Or maybe she wouldn't be able to believe it. Maybe that's what everyone was going through. What would happen when the truth finally hit them?

Later, as Mattie drifted off to sleep, she thought that the truth had come to Virgil. Through the thin wall she heard soft snuffling sounds—the noise of someone crying into a blanket. And still she hadn't found any words to tell him she was sorry.

7

✤♪✦♪✦♪✦♪✤

AS THE CAR ROLLED DOWN TOWARD THE
mining camp huddled in the narrow valley, Mattie
breathed deeply. The mountains smelled the way she
remembered from twelve Aprils spent there, a smell of
leaf mold and of thousands of violets and trilliums and
wood anemones blooming.

She thought about the cousins she was going to see—
Jimmy Dale who would be graduating from high school
in another month and for whom the army was waiting;
the twins, Kathy and Karen, who were close to Janie
Mae's age and who had an endless imagination for
games to be played; and Aunt Ida's babies from around
on Beaver Creek, a passel of diapered little ones Mattie
could never seem to keep straight. And there'd be Gran
and Gramps—Gran wiping her eyes on the tail of her
blue calico apron, even when she was happy, and
Gramps calling Mattie and Janie Mae "as fine a bunch
of boys as anybody ever grew," and wondering when
they'd be old enough to play professional baseball.

But when they pulled up in front of the fence surrounding the clean swept yard and she saw Gramps
crossing the porch, Mattie knew he'd forgotten all
about his trickster ways. He walked like an old man, his

head bowed and his shoulders bent in on his body as if a wind were blowing behind him. Mattie suddenly realized he was old, old enough that, as Mother often said, if it weren't for the war and every able-bodied person being needed to work at something useful, the coal company would let Gramps go.

The screen door opened again, and there was Gran. But Mattie had to look twice to be sure the tidy woman in laced-up black shoes and a gray silklike dress was really her grandmother. Where were the apron and flowered cotton dress? The soft slippers molded by much wear to the shape of her feet? Instead of the corner of her apron, Gran was dabbing at her eyes with a flowered handkerchief.

Mother was out of the car and fumbling with the latch on the gate. Then Daddy was beside her, pushing open the gate. Mother rushed up the wooden steps and put an arm around Gramps's stooped shoulders. Mattie saw Mother's back jerk with the sob that escaped from her, and when she saw Gramps lay his cheek against Mother's hair, she was glad Mother believed in hugging. She wondered how her grandparents would act toward Virgil. Even more, she wondered what Virgil was feeling now that he was back in the place that was most nearly home for him.

He climbed out of the far side of the car. Janie Mae had sat in the middle of the backseat for the entire trip so that Mattie and Virgil might each have a window. Ordinarily Mattie would have traded with her for part of the ride and would have insisted that Virgil let one of them have a turn at his window seat. But Virgil had sat unmoving for the entire six-hour drive. He had gazed at the mountains with their early spring hint of green as if he'd never seen mountains before. It was as if some stranger had stepped into Virgil's clothes and had ridden along to observe how everyone else responded to a death in the family, some stranger who knew their names but nothing else about them. So Mattie had remained by her window seat, looking out the window most of the time, too, but stealing glances at Virgil occasionally. She had no desire to sit in Janie Mae's seat and feel her body bump against Virgil as the car swung on the twisting road.

"Virgil?" Gran called. The voice that was accustomed to giving commands had a question in it. Mattie thought Gran, too, felt the strangeness of Virgil, felt the difference even with Virgil standing outside the gate.

All the adults turned to watch Virgil cross the open lawn and climb the steps to the porch. Gran wrapped her arms around him, but Virgil stood stiffly, so she stepped back from him and gave his shoulder a pat.

"Well, come in, come in," Gran said. "Reckon it's a little cool for standing on the porch."

Mattie and Janie Mae followed the adults and Virgil into the familiar room. Two double beds filled most of the room, their bulk separated by a low chest, usually covered with a scarf and family pictures. Today the top of the chest was raised and a dress in soft ivory lay across the bed.

"Why, Mom, that's your wedding dress," Mother said.

"Yes," Gran said, smoothing back a wisp of hair that had escaped the braids wound around her head, "that's what I aim to have Opal buried in."

Virgil looked interested for the first time. "Aw, Gran, she ain't big enough to fit into your dress."

All of Gran's daughters were shorter and smaller than she was, so none of them had been married in the dress with its yoke of lace where, in Gran and Gramps's wedding picture, a cameo lay like an Easter egg almost concealed by the ruffles. The cameo had been worn by Opal and Mother and Ida when they were married, and Mattie knew it lay now in the chest waiting for the weddings of the granddaughters.

"The size of the dress for a laying out don't matter much," Gran said in answer to Virgil. Then, as if suspecting he might not want to think about such things, she walked briskly to the kitchen. "Now, you all come on and get a bite to eat."

The table was covered with bowls of green beans, corn, and mashed potatoes; platters of chicken and sliced ham; and cakes and pies. Gramps looked at the food and shook his head. "Law, the neighbors that've been in!" He sank into a chair and waited while Gran filled a plate and placed it before him.

The mixed aromas of so much food made Mattie realize how hungry she was. They'd eaten only a piece of toast for breakfast and had stopped on the trip just long enough to fill the car with gasoline and to eat a candy bar. Now the five of them heaped their plates, then sat with Gramps around the table, Gran closest to the stove, her post during all their meals. Mattie often wondered how Gran stayed so energetic when she never seemed to eat, but Mother told her Gran ate all the time she was cooking. She never used recipes, just dumped things together until the dish tasted right to her. By the time she got a meal on the table, Mother figured Gran had eaten more than most people would ever put on their plates.

As Mattie ate, she stole glances into the parlor. The door, usually latched high up on its frame where none of the young grandchildren could reach, now stood open. Someone had wrapped flowers around the wire by which the picture of the Last Supper hung.

Gran nodded. "Some of the neighbors was over here first thing this morning. Aired out the parlor and got it cleaned up and proper-looking for a family with a burying." Gran rubbed the knuckles of her hands. "My rheumatism has eased up some, and I told them I could get the work done, but they said no, what're neighbors for if they can't help out in a time of trouble."

Although the house had only the kitchen and three other rooms, the parlor was saved for special occasions. Gran insisted that a house had to have someplace nice enough to receive the preacher. Ordinarily when the entire family was home at one time, they all crowded around the kitchen table or in the other front room where the two beds sat and the rockers were gathered by the fireplace.

After everyone had eaten, the adults got into the McDowells' car and drove off, "to take care of the arrangements," Gran explained. Virgil wandered outside to the backyard, and Mattie heard the sound of rocks hitting a tin can. She wondered if he wished he had his gun so he could fill the can with holes instead of just peppering it with stones. She and Janie Mae pulled out Gramps's worn checkerboard and pushed aside enough bowls to make room on the table for the game. The parlor waited with its overstuffed maroon furniture, but Mattie didn't think she'd be able to concentrate on moving her checker pieces if she sat in there.

It was late afternoon when the adults returned. Mattie hadn't seen Virgil since they had gone, and the ping of cans had stopped hours earlier.

Uncle Herbert, his wife Mildred, and Jimmy Dale and the twins came in soon after her parents got back. Aunt Mildred was carrying a pair of gray wool pants and a long-sleeved white shirt, clothes Jimmy Dale had outgrown a couple of years earlier.

"Where's Virgil?" Uncle Herbert asked.

They all looked at Mattie. She shrugged her shoulders. "I guess he's in the backyard."

Gran walked to the door. "Yoo hoo, Virgil," she called.

There was no answer.

"Maybe he's gone next door," Mother suggested.

Mattie shook her head. The adults didn't seem to know Virgil very well. "I bet he's up on the mountain," she said.

"Maybe somebody better go after him," Gran said. She looked at Daddy.

This time Daddy shook his head. "Let him be. He'll come back by supper time."

Daddy was right. Virgil walked in the door just as the family congregated once more to fill their plates from the abundant food. Mattie noticed that Virgil smelled of the outdoors, of the verdant aroma of the mountains. She looked quickly at him, expecting his face to be tear streaked. But his features were as they'd been for almost twenty-four hours now—like the mouth, nose, and eyes of a statue, placed in the right spots, perfectly proportioned, but not really belonging to a thinking and feeling human.

Aunt Mildred patted his shoulder awkwardly, and

Uncle Herbert shook his hand. Virgil barely responded. Jimmy Dale went on filling his plate, but his movements were jerky, as if he weren't certain he ought to be acting natural. Mattie knew how he felt. She still hadn't found words to tell Virgil she was sorry about the death of his mother, and that made her feel strange around him. It was as if her lack of communication had built a wall between them. She told herself that was silly—their usual conversations bordered on arguments. So why should she miss a closeness she'd never had? But maybe arguing was a special kind of communication, and maybe that was what she missed. However, she certainly couldn't start an argument with Virgil now—Gran would throw her out of the house.

Janie Mae and the twins were playing in the parlor. A burst of laughter came from the room, sounding tentative in the quiet kitchen, as if it were trying out the silence. Gran glanced in the girls' direction, then went back to filling Virgil's plate. Gran was acting strange, too. She still wore the gray dress and black-laced shoes, and she hadn't said a word to the girls in the parlor about staying off the furniture or not touching the stiffly starched runners beneath the lamps on the end tables.

Opal's body lay in the funeral home in Peak Town, twenty-three miles away. But the adults acted as though she was in the next room, watching to see how they'd react to her death.

8

LIFE IN GENERAL AND VIRGIL IN PARTICULAR
were as strange to Mattie next day as they had been the
day before. She moved from one room to another, not
knowing what she should be doing. Janie Mae had
spent the night with the twins, leaving Mattie without
an anchor. Neighbors drifted in and out with bowls and
platters of food and with words of sympathy. Virgil
disappeared after breakfast and stayed away until late
afternoon. Only Daddy's insistence that the boy
needed time alone kept Gran from going up on the
mountain to search for him.

Finally it was time to dress to go to the funeral home.
Virgil put on the gray wool pants and the white shirt.
Even though Jimmy Dale had outgrown the clothes
several years earlier, they still didn't fit Virgil's small
frame. But he hid the fact that the sleeves were too long
by rolling them to just below his elbow, and he pulled
a belt tightly about his waist to make the pants fit
passably.

Mother called Mattie aside. "I hate to ask you to do
this," she said, "but Aunt Ida would rather the twins
didn't go to the funeral home. And I feel the same way

about Janie Mae. Would you mind staying here with them this evening?"

Mattie breathed a sigh of relief. She had about run out of words of acknowledgment when people told her how sorry they were about her aunt. And she wasn't sure she wanted to spend the evening standing in a funeral home where an open casket lay.

When the others drove away, Mattie and the three little girls settled in the parlor with a box of paper dolls Kathy and Karen had brought. Although there were many childhood pastimes Mattie had outgrown, she still enjoyed paper dolls—though she certainly wouldn't admit it to anyone her age. There was something about dressing the dolls in outfit after outfit and maneuvering them about, imagining the mansions where they lived and the cars they drove—no gas rationing for paper dolls—that lifted Mattie out of the small mining-company house where she sat.

It was almost ten and the girls were beginning to yawn when Mattie heard the first car pull up in front of the house. "We'd better get this room cleaned up," she said, stuffing the paper dolls quickly into their box.

The parlor door to the porch, usually kept locked, was open, and adults and teenagers flooded through the room.

"I'll put a pot of coffee on, Mom," Mother said. "Everybody'll want a cup."

The adults talked lightly and laughed quickly, as if they were returning from a baseball game or from a wedding shower. Mattie looked about for Virgil. Would he be himself again, the way he'd always been before that telephone call two nights ago?

The house was full of cousins. Not Aunt Ida's babies,

who had been left with a neighbor. And not just Jimmy Dale and the twins. Second and third cousins were everywhere, laughing and calling to one another, asking about a schoolteacher or teasing one another about a boyfriend or a girlfriend. Mattie had been away not quite a year, and already she felt a stranger to the conversations around her.

When she had checked all the rooms and still hadn't found Virgil, she went to the front porch. The night was warm, with the soft feel of early spring. From near the creek, peepers called. Voices flowed from the house behind her, as if carried along on streams of light pouring from windows and doors. She perched on the top step and peered into the darkness.

Something moved at the edge of the lawn, and a shape stepped into a beam of light.

"Virgil," she called softly.

Virgil shielded his eyes with a hand, the way women did when they stood talking to one another in a sunny yard.

Mattie knew she was just a dark outline in the light spilling from the house. "It's me—Mattie," she said.

Virgil hesitated, looking around as if he'd like to find a place to hide. Then he walked slowly to the steps and sank down beside Mattie. He propped his elbows on his knees and lowered his face to his hands.

"I reckon that was the worse thing I've ever had to do," he said.

Mattie nodded. She'd known it would be bad.

Virgil raised his head and looked at Mattie. She could see only half his face, the part exposed by the light from the door. His visible eye reflected the light, but it looked empty, like the window of a deserted house.

The tuft of hair along Virgil's crown had come un-slicked again in spite of all Gran's efforts; and his chin, which always jutted out when he and Mattie argued, was a prominent part of his face this evening.

"You know what they do?" he asked.

Mattie shook her head wordlessly.

"They fix the dead person up real nice—at least, everybody said Mama looked nice—and lay them in a coffin. Then everybody walks by and looks down at them. Some people stand there a long time and some people just go by fast, like they really don't want to look but think they'll make somebody mad if they don't." Virgil shook his head. "I wouldn't of been mad if nobody looked. If I ever go to another funeral, I'm not going to even go close to the casket."

He turned away and stared toward the dark hills rising beyond the road. He gripped his left hand with his right and, slowly and methodically, popped each knuckle. Then he turned back to her.

"You know what was the worst thing about Mama?"

Once more Mattie shook her head. She knew Virgil really didn't want an answer. He just needed to talk to somebody and she was the one closest to hand. But it was okay. Maybe she couldn't tell him how sorry she was. Maybe she didn't even know how she felt about somebody in the family dying. But she could listen. She could listen hard.

"It was her mouth. It looked like it had never moved, like it had never been part of a living person. When Gran took me in that room and I first saw her there like that, I wanted to die, too. I didn't think I could stand to be alive with her just laying there so still. Then I saw her mouth, set hard with the lips stretched tight. Then

I knew. I knew it wasn't Mama laying there."

Mattie frowned. What did he mean it wasn't Opal? It had to be her. The rest of the family would have known. Was Virgil cracking up over all this? She leaned closer and peered at him in the dark, but his face was as unmovable as ever.

He gave his knuckles one extraloud pop and stood up. "I reckon that's what got me through the night." He looked down at Mattie. "Ever time I looked at that box, I just kept saying to myself, 'That's not Mama in there. She's done gone, gone wherever people go when they die. That's just something she left behind, something they put Gran's wedding dress on to make it look pretty.'"

He sat back down suddenly. "You know what I did then, Mattie? I went into the bathroom and locked the door. I sat on the edge of that toilet and cried." He looked cautiously at her.

Mattie laid a hand on Virgil's knee; the gray wool felt scratchy and more a part of winter and church than of Gran's front steps and spring. Virgil let her hand lie there.

"And, you know something? Crying felt good. Oh, it hurt, but it felt good, too. It was like a doctor had taken his knife and cut a big place out of my throat, a place that'd been hurting for days. It didn't come out easy, but once it was gone, I thought maybe I was going to live through this after all."

Now Virgil turned toward her and a grin lit the part of his face that showed. "Let's go get some of that food everybody's been bringing over. I feel like I haven't eaten for days."

Mattie grinned back. At least some of the old Virgil

had returned, the part that knew it had a stomach.

She stood beside him, and they started up the steps. Before they crossed the porch, they heard the gate creak.

"Would one-a you kids be Virgil?" a voice called to them.

9

MATTIE AND VIRGIL SLOWLY TURNED TO FACE the stranger in Gran's yard. Although Mattie knew the man could see only their silhouettes against the light spilling from the house, she saw him clearly. He had small, dark eyes that glinted in the light and a mustache covering his upper lip. His chin was small and receded into his neck. Mattie thought he looked as if he'd forgotten to grow a chin and remembered it so late that it never quite caught up with the rest of his face.

"Can you tell me whereabouts I might find Virgil Davis?" the man asked.

Mattie looked at Virgil. He was staring openmouthed at the stranger. Then he swallowed and stepped to the edge of the porch. "I'm Virgil," he said.

The man pulled a dirty handkerchief from his back pocket and noisily blew his nose. Then he advanced slowly toward the porch. "Well, Virge, I'm sure glad to see you after all these years. Me and you have lost the best woman there ever was."

"Who are you?" Virgil asked, his voice barely audible above the call of the peepers.

"Why, Virge, you don't know your own pap? I'm Jesse, Jesse Davis."

Mattie leaned for support against the door frame. Jesse Davis, after all these years!

Virgil stood straight. "What do you want?" he asked.

Jesse stopped. He had one foot on the bottom step. He looked up at Virgil, shading his eyes with his hand, just as Virgil had done half an hour earlier. "What do you mean, 'What do you want?' I come to pay my respects." The man puckered his lips together and lowered his gaze.

"I don't reckon Mama needs something now she didn't have from you when she was alive."

Once more the man peered up at Virgil's dark shape. "Now, Virge," he began in a whining voice.

"My name is Virgil."

Jesse put his hands in his pockets and smiled. "All right, Virgil. I reckon we can be formal. And you don't have to call me Pap. You can just call me Jesse." The man seemed to measure Virgil with his eyes. "You ain't very big for your age—that'd be nearly thirteen, wouldn't it? But you look healthy and strong enough. I reckon now that you'll be living with me, you'll be right handy around the place. Yep, right handy."

The man nodded toward the house. "You just give my respects to the rest of the family." Then he turned and shuffled out of the yard, the gate creaking shut behind him.

Virgil stood unmoving, staring into the darkness where the man had vanished. Finally he turned and faced Mattie. "What did he mean, I'd be living with him?"

Mattie shrugged. "I don't know, Virgil. I wouldn't pay any attention to him."

But Virgil couldn't dismiss the man so easily. "He's

my dad, and maybe I have to do what he says now."

"Maybe you have to do what who says, Virgil?" Daddy asked from the other side of the screen door.

Virgil ran one hand through his hair, further disturbing the cowlick which stuck straight up. "Aw, nothing, Uncle Omer. I was just talking."

"Seems a strange remark for idle conversation," Daddy said, as he pushed the door open and walked out onto the porch. "What about it, Mattie?"

Virgil looked quickly at her. There was something in his eyes she hadn't seen before, a sort of pleading.

She smiled at Daddy. "We were just talking about school," she said, crossing her fingers behind her back, hoping he'd think she'd been trying to divert Virgil's attention from the funeral home.

Daddy nodded. "Well, come on into the kitchen. It's time you two got some food in your stomachs."

The rest of the evening was spent in an easy atmosphere of family camaraderie. If Virgil was worried about what Jesse had said to him, he didn't show it. Instead, he seemed to be his usual self—laughing and talking to everyone, admiring Jimmy Dale, and boasting to his other cousins of all he'd seen in that strange town of Oak Ridge.

Mattie fell asleep thinking Virgil was back to normal and being glad despite herself.

Next day when the family arrived at the small church set against the side of the mountain, the building was already full. People who couldn't get in stood outdoors near the windows to hear Brother Carroll preach the last words over Sister Opal Turner Davis—who, since she had died suddenly in an accident, was probably taken in her sins and in need of many words of prayer.

Mattie grabbed Janie Mae's hand and slipped into one of the pews reserved for family members. Everyone else walked slowly to the open casket standing near the pulpit. Mattie watched Virgil's back stiffen. She wished she could have taken his hand and led him like she did Janie Mae, but Gran was keeping him close to her. As he turned, Mattie saw his face. He hadn't really looked at Opal, she was sure. His face was set as carefully as Mother and Aunt Ida had set their hair. He was probably ready for whatever Brother Carroll had to say.

And Brother Carroll had plenty to say. As soon as the last wheezy strains of the organ died out, he stood up, mopped his face, and leaned heavily on the lectern. Mattie wondered that he could breath. Rolls of flesh hung over his collar, and his face was red above his white suit. But from somewhere inside his vast frame breath came, propelling words out of him and flinging them over the heads of those gathered in the pews, to drift along the breeze surrounding those who stood listening beneath the windows. Mattie felt as if his voice were a strong river current sweeping them all away. She gripped the back of the pew in front of her and struggled to keep her own breathing steady. Everyone around her seemed willing to ride the current. They swayed with the voice, heads nodding, their own amens like pebbles tossed into the stream.

Mattie was close enough to the casket that the scent of flowers filled her nostrils each time she breathed— violets from the creek banks, tall purple irises from lawn borders, yellow, lemony-smelling trilliums from the mountainsides. She might have imagined she was up on the mountain, but the splintery feel of the wooden pew kept her anchored in the church.

Finally the organ began to wheeze once more, and the high- and low-pitched voices of the congregation blended in the strains of "Beautiful River":

"Shall we gather at the river,
Where bright angel feet have trod;
With its crystal tide forever
Flowing by the throne of God?"

Mattie joined in, singing, "Yes, we'll gather at the river, the beautiful, the beautiful river," just as she'd always sung it in church, ever since she'd been old enough to separate the words from the flow of adult voices. But there was a difference in the singing this time—this time they were singing a last hymn for somebody who had been a part of her life. Maybe she'd never had a chance to know Aunt Opal well, but the woman lying there at the front of the church was a part of her because of the blood that had flowed through her veins, a blending of Gran and Gramps's blood, the same as that flowing now through Mother's veins, through the veins of all the Turners. Yes, even through Virgil's veins.

The rest of Virgil's blood came from Jesse. Mattie shuddered as she thought of the whining man. She hadn't seen him in the church, but there were a lot of people outside.

Virgil rose with the rest of the congregation and filed out of the church and up the hillside. They walked slowly, allowing the pallbearers time to maneuver the casket around bends in the well-worn path. Mattie thought they would have walked just as slowly had there been no pallbearers in front. It was as if each footfall repeated, "This is the last thing we can do for Opal, the last thing we can do for Opal." Mattie was

surprised to find that, although everyone looked sol-
emn, the sadness that had surrounded them for days
was gone. It was as if they truly had done all they could
for Opal, had fulfilled some sort of communal obliga-
tion, and were now ready to get on with their lives.

She watched Virgil standing by the open grave, Gran
close beside him. The link connecting them was being
buried. Virgil leaned his head against Gran's shoulder,
closing the space left vacant.

Words of the Twenty-third Psalm seemed to echo
still from the mountainsides as the crowd made its way
back down the path: ". . . though I walk through the
valley of the shadow of death . . ." Death had shad-
owed their valley, but now Mattie felt only life surrounding them. The valley spread before them was
green with early spring, and the people she had known
since her birth filled that valley.

Kathy and Karen took Janie Mae by the hand and
skipped ahead, the need for solemnity gone. Mattie had
watched Janie Mae through the burial, but her sister
had seemed calm, as if she were attending just another
church service. Even the cemetery hadn't bothered her,
although Mattie couldn't look at the tombstones without thinking of the rock they'd propped at the head of
the rabbit's grave. Maybe seeing something alive one
minute and dead the next gave a sense of the finality
of death, a sense that a seven-year-old couldn't grasp
otherwise. Whatever the reason, Mattie was glad Janie
Mae seemed unaffected.

Mattie was walking down the hill beside Daddy
when Sonny Jenkins caught up with them.

"Omer, I can't tell you and Lucy and your girls how
sorry I am about your loss."

Daddy nodded.

"Guess the whole camp will miss her."

Daddy nodded again.

"Reckon just because we haven't seen much of her lately don't make losing her any easier to take."

Daddy took Mattie's hand. She wondered if he was all nodded out by now, because he just smiled politely at the sheriff.

The sheriff clapped Daddy on the shoulder. "Well, now, maybe me and you can talk some business."

"Business?" Daddy said.

"Yeah, you know." The sheriff looked furtively over his shoulder. "Police business."

"Sorry, Sonny, I don't know any police business."

"Sure, sure. I know you're not supposed to talk about your job. But just as one professional to another"— Sonny puffed out his chest—"how about letting me in on some of the new FBI methods?"

"Sonny, I'd help you if I could, but I don't know any more about the FBI than Mattie here." Daddy gave her hand an extra squeeze. She smiled up at him.

Sonny removed his hand from Daddy's shoulder. "I reckon they trained you too good, Omer. Can't even help out an old friend of the family." He put his hands in his pockets and hung his head.

"Now, don't take it personally. Even if I were an FBI man, I wouldn't be allowed to talk about such things."

The sheriff's face lit up and he smiled broadly, showing the gap where two teeth had been knocked out the first time he ran for sheriff. Mattie had heard it said that some people bought offices in Lloyd County with folding money, but Sonny Jenkins had bought his position with two of his teeth. When he'd gone right on fighting, blood spurting from his mouth, the other fellow had lost heart, lost the fight, and dropped out of the race. Sonny hadn't had any opposition since.

Now he seemed about ready to laugh. "Omer, that's a good one. Even if you was with the FBI, huh? Yep, they trained you good. Reckon if they ever need any more men, they'll know where they can come to get the best ones. Yep, you're a good one all right."

Daddy looked at Mattie and raised his eyebrows.

Sonny walked on down the mountainside chuckling to himself.

Later, with the family crowded into Gran's small kitchen once more eating from the seemingly endless supply of bowls and platters, Virgil came in dressed in blue jeans and shirt. His hair was less tidy than Mother and Gran had attempted to keep it for the past few days. He looked perfectly normal again to Mattie.

Gran had carefully hung her gray dress back into the clothes press which stood along the bedroom wall. Now she wore faded blue calico, the small flowers made indistinguishable by numerous washings. The ever-present apron was once more tied about her waist. She, too, looked to Mattie like her usual self. And when, the supper dishes finished, Gran walked to the back door and flung the dishwater in a wide arc, Mattie felt she had her grandmother back again. It was one of the things she most admired about Gran, the way she could empty the dishpan and never get a drop of water on herself or on the porch.

Having Gran and Virgil back to normal was all fine, but Mattie wasn't sure how happy she was later that evening when Mother told her Gran and Gramps would be returning to Oak Ridge for a while with them. Gran, with her stern ways, was nice to be around for a few days, but Mattie wasn't sure how long she could take living with her. Besides, where would they put Gran and Gramps in their small house?

She was afraid she knew the answer to that question.

10

MATTIE WAS RIGHT ABOUT WHERE GRAN AND
Gramps would sleep.

"It's only for a few days, Mattie," Mother said, as she
spread sheets over the stiff canvas cots they had bor-
rowed from a neighbor. "Besides, it'll be fun. You and
Janie Mae can pretend you're camping."

Mattie thought camping under the stars on the hard
cots might be okay, but sleeping crowded into the tiny
living room with Virgil nearby on the sofa wasn't her
idea of camping out. Still, Janie Mae seemed to enjoy
it. And the dream that sent her into terror didn't recur
during that week. Mattie was glad, because after putting up with Gran all day, she figured she needed all the
sleep she could get.

Gran was a demanding boarder. The warm spell that
had begun while the family was in Kentucky continued. "Reckon I'll just help you with your spring
cleaning while I'm here, Lucy," Gran said one morning.

"Now, Mom, we're not going to worry about any
such thing this week. We brought you and Pop down
here to give you a chance to relax and get over all
you've been through."

"Pshaw, I reckon the best way to get over something

is to stay busy. We'll start with the curtains, and while they're drying, we'll get all these windows washed."

Mattie picked up her books and started out the door.

Gran stopped her with one piercing look. "Reckon Mattie here could stay home today and help us?"

Mother looked up from her coffee cup. "No, afraid not, Mom. The most important thing my girls do is get to school each day." She smiled at Mattie.

Mattie hurried out the door. She knew Gran, never one to admit defeat, would save some work for her. But at least she could escape for now.

Later, after school, she discovered she was right about the work. As she and Janie Mae and Virgil walked down the lane in the afternoon sun, she saw the wooden curtain-stretcher frames set up in the yard with the curtains drying on them. Janie Mae saw them, too, and hurried ahead. She was planning to crawl beneath the tentlike structure, probably with a doll or two, and play there for the rest of the afternoon. Mattie had done that herself for years. Even after she had outgrown dolls, she would often sit in the gauzy light that came through the curtains, the starchy smell of freshly laundered fabric surrounding her.

In their house in the mining camp, Mother had set up the curtain stretchers in the dining room, an area used only for Sunday dinner and special family occasions. Here in their tiny Oak Ridge house, the outdoors was the only safe place for the frames, the only spot large enough that no one would stick himself on the hundreds of needles projecting from the wooden frames. Mother stretched the curtains tightly over the frame, securing the flimsy material upon the needle ends. Sometimes Mattie helped her. Always she was careful to spread her fingers on each side of the sharp points as she pushed the fabric tight.

Gramps, in a kitchen chair, leaned against an oak tree. "Howdy, boys," he said, as Mattie and Virgil caught up with Janie Mae.

"Hi, Gramps." Janie Mae smiled at him.

"How many home runs did you get today?" he asked, setting his chair down on all four legs.

"Gramps, they don't let first-graders play baseball," Janie Mae said.

"Don't let you play baseball? Why, what's your ma thinking, sending you to such a school?"

Janie Mae put her hand over her mouth and giggled.

Gramps turned to Mattie and Virgil. "And how about you fellas?"

Virgil puffed out his chest. "I hit so many home runs, they had to call the game. Why, I hit those balls so far, they're probably still traveling."

Gramps whooped with delight. Then he leaned toward Mattie and arched an eyebrow. "And you? As fine a strapping boy as I've ever seen. Did you outplay them all?"

But Mattie was suddenly angry. Why did it always have to be *boys* who were so special?

She jutted out her jaw. "I caught two long fly balls. But I did it because I'm a girl, and I can keep my eye on the ball, and I can jump high." She stood with her feet apart and her fists against her hips.

Gramps nodded at her as he leaned his chair back against the tree. "Well, now, Mattie lass, I guess you're right. We've got some women in this family who are fine as they come. And I reckon you're going to be another one of them." He smiled. "Reckon it's time I opened my eyes."

Mattie was immediately sorry for her angry words, but before she could say anything more, Gran came down the steps, the empty clothes basket on her arm.

"There you are, Mattie, just in time." She handed the basket to Mattie. "The things on the line are dry. Reckon you can dampen them and maybe get them ironed before supper."

Well, Mattie thought, Gran could have given her a chance to eat a snack. But then, she guessed she was lucky to have escaped all day.

Virgil passed by her. "Girls' work," he said out of the corner of his mouth.

She pulled loose the clothespins, folded the sun-shine-smelling laundry, and laid it in the basket. It was a pleasant enough job, and her anger melted away.

Gramps ambled over to join her. If he had been hurt by her earlier remark, he had quickly dismissed it. Now he was his usual self.

"Law, the work that old woman can think up." He chuckled. "She don't want any menfolks in her way when she's housecleaning, so I've been sitting under that tree all day. She's had Lucy up and down that ladder, washing ever window in sight. Reckon we'll have to wear sunglasses with all the light coming in those windows now."

When Mattie went into the house with the clothes basket, Mother was peeling potatoes. She looked glad to have a sitting-down job. Gran was rubbing an oily cloth up and down the legs of the lamp table. Her back was straight and she looked as fresh as she had when

Mattie left home that morning. Mattie wondered at her resilience. A month ago her rheumatism had been so bad she could barely use her hands, and now look at her. It was almost as if Opal's death had poured strength into her.

Mattie took the ironing board from behind the door and set it in the middle of the living room.

"Come sit down a minute before you start that," Mother said. "Tell me about your day."

Gran paused in her polishing. Mattie didn't let her eyes meet her grandmother's as she poured a glass of milk and slid into a chair at the table. Mother laid down the knife and rested her chin on her hand, ready for their after-school conversation.

"Pshaw," Gran said, "no wonder you two never get your work done." She picked up the bottle of furniture oil and marched into Mattie and Janie Mae's bedroom, where they could hear her attacking the dresser.

Mattie and Mother looked at each other and laughed. You're lucky you had school today, Mother mouthed, rolling her eyes toward the bedroom. Mattie wanted to remind Mother she was the one who'd said a few inconveniences would be fun, but she thought such a remark might sound a little smart alecky, and she didn't want to lose her chief ally.

By the time supper was on the table, Mattie had pressed the towels and T-shirts Mother and Gran had laundered and had ironed the starched kitchen curtains so their edges lay in stiff ruffles. She started to put away the ironing board.

"Reckon you'd better leave it up," Gran said. "If we take the curtains off the frames soon as we eat, we'll get them ironed and back at the windows before dark."

"Now, Mom," Mother said, "we'll have all day tomorrow to do that. What can't be done by supper time always keeps just fine till another day."

"Well . . ." Gran looked as if she might argue the point, but Mattie quickly tucked the ironing board into its spot behind the door.

When they turned on the radio to catch the evening news, the family was glad they'd stopped work. The gravelly voice of the announcer drove all thoughts of housecleaning out of their heads.

"This is a black day for the United States and for the world," the voice said. "The President of the United States, Franklin Delano Roosevelt, died this afternoon at Warm Springs, Georgia. Tributes from around the world . . ."

Static drowned the rest of the man's words, but the group around the table knew what he had said. They all looked at their plates for a few moments. Then one by one they raised their heads and looked questioningly into each other's eyes.

Gramps shook his head. "We're not likely to see the likes of him again soon. Nope, there was a big man who cared about all the little men."

"I reckon he was the best president the United States ever had," Virgil said.

Mattie looked at him in surprise. "When did you decide that?" she asked. Most people she knew in the mountains were Republicans, and even if they admired Roosevelt, they kept their feelings to themselves. Except Gramps, who said whatever he wanted and left people to decide for themselves whether he was serious or joking.

"I reckon I've always known it," Virgil said.

Gran dabbed at her eyes with the corner of her apron. Mattie wondered if she was sad about the president, or if she was remembering that other death a few days earlier. The words from the closing hymn flooded into her mind. "Yes, we'll gather at the river, the beautiful, the beautiful river . . ." Death, she supposed, was the same whether you were president of a powerful country or just a woman from a mining camp. There would be a casket and flowers and, finally, a cemetery and everyone going away with a sense of relief that they'd done what they could to honor the dead one. Being famous didn't protect you at all.

Early the next week Gran began to talk of going back home. Mattie figured she'd cleaned everything she could get her hands on in their home and had to go find another challenge. She felt sorry for Aunt Ida and Uncle Herbert and their families.

Daddy got extra gas coupons, available for emergencies, from the rationing office at work and was ready to leave with Gran and Gramps as Mattie, Janie Mae, and Virgil were going off to school. Gramps clapped each of them on the back. "Now, you boys—and you, too, Mattie lass—never mind about all them books. Get out on the baseball diamond and learn all you can." His eyes twinkled, and Mattie thought he looked more rested than he had for a long time. Maybe a week of sitting under the trees watching Gran work was just what he needed. Now he'd have to go back down into the mines and dig out the hard black coal that kept so much of the country going. Mattie kissed his sunken cheek, the stubble of beard scratching her lips.

Gran kissed Janie Mae on the cheek. Then she patted Virgil's cowlick into place. "Now you mind Lucy and

Omer and don't be getting into any trouble," she said.

Virgil nodded. Even though Gran had recovered from the bout with rheumatism that had caused Virgil to come to Oak Ridge, no mention was made of his returning to Kentucky. Maybe the grown-ups had decided he didn't need to change schools again this year. Anyway, Mattie was grateful that Jesse hadn't shown up, but she was sure Virgil still worried about what the man had said. She noticed that each day when the mail came, he glanced quickly through the letters.

Now with her grandparents leaving Virgil in Oak Ridge, she could see the rest of April and all of May stretching in front of her. If someone had told her last month that Virgil would stay so long, she would have jumped off the roof. Somehow now, she couldn't even work up a good shudder at the thought. She hoped she wasn't going soft with age.

As Mattie started out the door, Gran called her back. "Mattie, you being my firstborn granddaughter, I reckon I ought to go ahead and give you this."

Gran reached into the worn black handbag she always carried. Then she lifted Mattie's hand, palm up, and laid the cameo in it.

Mattie looked at the ivory-colored raised profile of a woman against the black background and at her own pink palm beneath it. This jewel had hung around Gran's neck and then around the necks of Lucy and Ida and Opal on their wedding days. The chain that held it was delicate, but it bound generations of women together. And now Gran was giving it to her. Mattie closed her fingers over the cameo. She'd share it with her cousins and Janie Mae when they got married.

Gran snapped her handbag shut. "Reckon we'd better be on our way," she said, and she walked briskly out the door. This time it was Mother who dabbed her eyes with the end of her apron.

By evening the warm spell of early April had been blown away by a strong wind out of the east. "Means a cold night," Mother said with a shiver. "Wish I'd had Omer lay a fire."

Mattie touched the cameo beneath her dress where it lay like an ordinary stone against her chest. Mother had let her wear it to school, just this once, she said, provided Mattie kept it hidden. Her fingers felt the ridges, and she could see in her mind the strong profile.

Shucks, she thought, I've watched Daddy build fires lots of times. No reason why I can't do it.

She went to the kindling box behind the stove, but it contained nothing except newspapers, the headlines still inky black with news of Roosevelt's death. Mattie knew enough about fire-building to know she'd need kindling to catch the quick flames from the paper and to sustain the heat long enough to ignite the stubborn coal. She straightened her back. I've watched Daddy split kindling plenty of times, she thought.

She carried the empty box outside. With the sun almost down, the wind was rising. The evening felt more like fall than spring, like the time of year when heavy sweaters began to feel good and when her thoughts could turn to Christmas and to the warm house with everyone gathered around the stove. But in spite of the cold, the air smelled of spring. Mattie sniffed deeply and recognized the sweet smell of poplar blossoms blooming out of sight in the tops of tall trees behind the house. It was one of the secret smells she loved, one that no one else ever mentioned and that she thought belonged only to her, as did the heady aroma of a field of corn in full tassel.

Beneath the porch she found the axe leaning against a pile of wood. She selected a couple of short wide boards, scraps from some building project, and carried them to a stump in the yard. When Daddy split lumber scraps, he steadied the board with one hand while the other hand effortlessly swung the axe into the wood.

At least, the swing had always looked effortless.

Now, as Mattie attempted to copy his manner, she realized that the axe was heavier than it looked. She needed both hands on it. But when she let go of the piece of wood, it tumbled off the stump. Well, she thought, a plain old board isn't going to get the best of me.

She went back under the house and brought out two logs which she laid close together on the stump. Then she wedged the scrap of lumber between them. With both hands on the handle, she lifted the axe behind her back and swung with all her strength, bringing her body along behind the axe in the follow-through motion she'd learned to use with a bat.

The axe bit sharply into the stump.

Mattie frowned as she worked the axe free. There was more to this kindling-splitting business than met the eye.

But she wasn't about to give up. Once more she lifted the heavy tool over her shoulder. This time she kept her eyes on the target, just as she kept her eye on a softball barreling across home plate. Her hand-eye coordination didn't fail her, but the axe barely bit into the piece of lumber. If Daddy had been swinging the axe, it would have gone straight down the grain, splitting the wood neatly into two halves.

Once more Mattie worked the blade loose.

As she again hefted the axe to her shoulder, she heard the door slam. Then Virgil descended the steps, each footfall a two-part harmony of heel then toe.

11

"RECKON YOU'RE TRYING TO DO MEN'S work," Virgil said, as he reached the bottom step.

Mattie gritted her teeth and put all her strength into her shoulders as she brought the axe down on the lumber. Once more the blade sank into the wood, but again it didn't split it.

She felt Virgil's presence behind her, the same way she felt Mrs. Gwen's eyes on her when she struggled with a difficult math problem. She always knew Mrs. Gwen was watching for errors so she could help Mattie correct them, which was what teachers were supposed to do—even if it made students uneasy. But she didn't need any correction from Virgil.

"What I need is a smaller piece of wood," she said.

Virgil laughed.

Mattie ignored him as she selected a shorter board. She secured it between the two logs and once more swung the axe. Again she was rewarded only by the thud of blade sinking into soft wood. Maybe lumber split only in the cold snappy air of winter!

She loosened the axe blade and leaned the tool against the stump. "I don't need kindling anyway," she said.

"Then I reckon we don't need a fire," Virgil said.

Mattie turned her back on him. When she was half-way to the door, she heard the sharp crack of a piece of wood splitting. She peeked over her shoulder. Virgil was tossing a splint to one side. Then he hefted the axe once more, swung it easily, and another crack echoed through the chilly evening.

"It's all in the wrist," he called, but she was taking the steps two at a time, not looking back.

The fire that heated the small house that evening was the last they would need for a while. By the time Daddy returned from Kentucky, spring had reasserted itself, and during the next few weeks afternoon temperatures crept into the eighties.

Like most of the plant workers, Daddy worked during the days one week, during the evenings the next, and at night the third week. One Saturday morning when he came off the night shift, he was smiling. "As soon as I sleep a couple of hours, I have a surprise for everybody. Lucy, why don't you and the girls pack a picnic?"

"Where are we going?" Mattie asked Mother as the two of them assembled flour, sugar, shortening, and eggs for a cake.

"I don't have any idea, but with gas rationing and all the trips we've had to make lately, it can't be very far." Mother looked as mystified as Mattie felt.

By the time Daddy woke up, Mother, Mattie, and Janie Mae had sliced bologna and made sandwiches, boiled and deviled eggs, prepared a bowl of potato salad, and baked, cooled, and frosted the cake. Virgil had vanished when he had seen the activity in the kitchen.

Daddy sniffed appreciatively as he came down the hall. "Well," he said, stretching his arms over his head, "that sure worked. Now we'll have a good meal and sit around here all afternoon."

"Daddy!" Mattie and Janie Mae cried out together.

Mother arched one eyebrow as she looked at him. "Omer McDowell, if you've . . ."

"It's awful what a fella has to resort to to get fed nowadays," he said. But Mattie knew from the crinkles around his eyes that he wasn't going to be able to tease them much longer.

"Okay, Daddy," she said, "where are we going?"

He grinned. "I'll tell you on the way. But you might want to take a bathing suit."

Mattie could hardly believe her ears. Just to be going on a picnic was enough—but to be going where there was a place to swim! She wondered if she'd been good enough to deserve all this at one time. Of course, having to put up with Virgil for nearly two months should have made her eligible for something special. At the moment she even felt good toward him.

"Somebody better tell Virgil to get his swim trunks," she called as she headed into the bedroom.

Virgil was just coming through the front door. There were damp spots on his clothes.

"Yep, go find a pair of trunks, Virgil," Daddy said.

"We never used them back home," Virgil said. "Just jumped in the creek in whatever we had on—if there were any girls around." He grinned, and Mattie wondered what he'd been up to that put him in such a good mood. Ever since Aunt Opal's death he had been like somebody pretending to be Virgil, somebody who just didn't quite understand how Virgil worked. Today he seemed to remember how he'd always been.

Daddy nodded knowingly. Mother pointed toward the bedroom. "There'll definitely be girls around today, so you'd better find something."

Mattie pulled out her old suit and Janie Mae's from the back of the drawer where they'd stayed all winter. Sure hope they still fit, she thought. All the clothes she'd put on this spring, things she'd worn comfortably last fall, had felt as if they belonged to somebody a size smaller. Mother had looked at her in despair. "Maybe your clothes won't choke you before school's out," she had said. Mattie had studied her reflection in the mirror, turning her side to it and puffing out her chest. That didn't help. She was getting longer arms and a bigger waist. Maybe Gramps should go on calling her a boy. It didn't look as if she would ever take after Mother, who was small, with curves in all the right places and had the kind of shape the movies showed the GIs pinning up in their barracks. Day by day Mattie realized she was looking more and more like Gran.

When the family stepped out on the porch, Mattie saw the reason behind Virgil's damp clothes. The car shone as brightly as the spring day.

Daddy slapped Virgil across the back. "What a fine thing to think about doing. Now this'll be the most stylish picnic a family ever went on."

Never mind that she and Mother and Janie Mae had worked all morning in the kitchen so it'd also be the tastiest picnic a family ever went on. But it was such a nice day, Mattie couldn't hold the mean thought in her mind for very long, and she climbed into the middle of the backseat, letting Janie Mae and Virgil have the preferred window seats.

"Now, Omer, tell us where we're going," Mother said, as the car crossed the one-lane plank bridge spanning Clinch River. Mattie opened her eyes. She always closed them when they traveled that bridge. As much as she loved to swim, she didn't like to look at the water swirling beneath.

"Well, if I'd let you out right here and you'd waded upstream about two miles, you'd be there," Daddy said, the mysterious smile still playing on his face.

They turned onto a dirt road which wound between fields. Farmers wearing straw hats walked behind mules, breaking the ground with plows that lurched through the clay soil. "We're almost there," Daddy said, "almost to Fred's."

"Fred's," Mother said. "You mean . . ."

Daddy nodded. "That's right. Uncle Glenn's oldest daughter. We lost touch with each other after Uncle Glenn died."

"But how did you find her?"

"One of the fellows at work lives on the farm next to hers. He happened to mention to her a few days ago that he worked with a McDowell, and when Fred found out it was me, well, she sent word by him that I was to get right out to see her, and to bring with me all the kit and caboodle of family I'd built up since she saw me sixteen or seventeen years ago."

Mother nodded. "Sounds as if she hasn't changed. But what's she doing out here on a farm?"

"Just that, far as I can figure out. Just farming, out here by herself. And this must be it," Daddy said, as he pulled under a shade tree in front of a square frame house.

A woman stepped out the front door, yanking an

apron from around her waist and flapping it menacingly. "Scat, get away," she yelled in a booming voice.

Mattie was more than willing to do as she said. Then
she saw a chicken spread its wings and fly off the porch,
and the woman descended the steps, a wide grin splitting her face as she rushed toward the car. "Get out, get
out," she boomed. Mattie began to understand why
Fred lived in the country.

Fred threw an arm around each of them as he or she
emerged from the car, but her heartiest greeting was
saved for Daddy. She engulfed him in a bear hug. "If
I'd known you were so close all this time. . ." She
shook her head. "And you work in that there Oak
Ridge?"

"Yep," he said. "Been there almost a year now."

"Well, I hope you-uns are doing something makes it
worthwhile what the government did to folks here-
abouts. Taking all that land away from families that've
farmed it for generations." Fred looked menacingly at
Daddy, as if he were partly responsible for the misery
her neighbors had suffered. "I was just lucky to live
over on the side of the river," she said.

Then she laughed loudly. "Well, I'm forgetting my
manners. Come in, come in."

To Mattie her words sounded more like an order
than an invitation.

They followed Fred into the cavelike darkness of the
house, across a living room crammed with overstuffed
furniture and a large black upright piano covered with
more pictures, books, and dusty plants than Mattie had
ever before seen gathered in one spot. Then they entered a big, square kitchen—the room where Fred obvi-

ously lived. A black stove stood at one end, a well-worn wooden table filled the middle of the room, and a rocking chair stood in front of a window. Mattie thought of their own small kitchen and the table that sat half in the living room. Living in a real house must be near heaven.

"Let me get everybody a drink of spring water," Fred boomed, in what seemed to be her natural voice. "I just brought in a fresh bucketful."

The water was cold and sweet tasting when Mattie put her lips to the metal dipper. It made her think of sinking into a lake.

Fred seemed to read her mind. "Now, if you young-uns brought some swim trunks, we'll just mosey down to the river."

"And the girls and I packed a picnic lunch," Mother said, heading back out to the car.

"You didn't need to go to no such trouble," Fred said. "Why, I've been known to cook for me and the dogs at least once a week." She laughed heartily—even more heartily than she spoke, Mattie thought and slapped a callused palm against her thigh.

Clinch River rolled gently past Fred's farmland. Even with the waters high from spring rains, large rocks were visible in it. It reminded Mattie of an extra-wide mountain stream. She wondered at the power of the river, at the fury it was said to have unleashed in the past—a fury which Norris Dam now held in check. And Norris Dam, her parents had told her, was one of the reasons Oak Ridge had been built. The electricity the dam provided made possible the thousands of houses the government had built in the valley. It kept the lights running twenty-four hours a day at the large plants where thousands of people did whatever they did around the clock.

Mattie stuck one toe into the water. It was as cold as the water she'd sipped in Fred's kitchen.

Fred laughed when she saw Mattie shiver. "I don't blame you, child. When they run those generators at Norris, they pull the coldest water off the bottom of that lake and send it down here to us. Then there's all them springs along the way, just like mine, feeding more cold water into the stream as it rushes by. Why, even on the hottest day of summer, your arm turns blue up to your elbow if you stick a finger in this river."

But Mattie was determined to swim even if she turned blue up to her eyebrows. She held her nose and plunged in. Her chest felt as if a giant had pressed it between his hands. She came up gasping.

"How is it, Mattie," Daddy called.

"Oh, it's wonderful," she shouted above the chattering of her teeth. "Everybody come on in."

"I'll just spread the lunch out," Mother said.

"And I'll help Lucy," Fred said with another burst of laughter.

Janie Mae eased into the water. She had brought an empty lard can, and she sat down in the shallows and began sorting through the pebbles.

"Well, Virgil, guess we can't let Mattie show us up," Daddy said, as he plunged in.

Mattie noticed that Virgil, for all his talk about boys being superior to girls, didn't look quite convinced. Finally, though, he held his nose and jumped into the water where Mattie and Daddy were paddling about. He came up wide-eyed and sputtering.

"Just the right temperature, isn't it?" Mattie flashed a smile at her cousin. Would Virgil admit the water was too cold for boys?

"Just right," Virgil agreed. He wiped the hair out of his eyes and stretched out on his back. Immediately he began sinking, and he flailed his arms and kicked his legs to stay afloat.

"Relax," Daddy told him. "The water will help support you."

Mattie flopped onto her back. Her body floated easily with just an occasional kick to bring her legs back near the surface.

"See how Mattie does it," Daddy said.

Virgil sank once again.

This time Daddy laughed. "Don't worry about it. When you get older and get a little fat on your body, it'll be easier. I guess that's one place the women have us beat. They're just naturally better floaters than we are."

Virgil made one more effort. Mattie could see the determination on his face. No girl was going to beat him at anything. But she knew when she saw his jaw tense that he was too stiff to float. Down he went once more.

"Tilt your head back and pull your chest up when you feel yourself sinking," she coached him. But Virgil turned onto his stomach and paddled away.

Well, thought Mattie, I ought to have told him it's all in the wrist.

12

SCHOOL ON MONDAY MORNING STARTED OFF badly. With only a few weeks remaining before summer vacation, Mattie had hoped the uneasy peace between Eddie and Virgil would continue. Since Opal's death, Eddie had backed off from Virgil, almost as if he were in awe of someone who had lost his mother. But this morning he was waiting inside the door when Mattie and Virgil entered the school building.

"It's gonna be today," he said, rocking from his heels to his toes.

"Suits me," Virgil said.

"Meet me behind the ball field, at the edge of the woods, right after school."

Virgil looked him over from head to foot. "Reckon all your bodyguards'll be able to make it, too?"

Mattie nearly burst out laughing at the look on Eddie's face. He wasn't used to having people challenge him.

But he recovered quickly and puffed out his chest. "Don't need anybody there but you and me. You leave Mattie behind and I'll manage to lose my buddies."

As they walked down the hall, Virgil clenched his jaw, but his eyes had a special light in them. "Okay, you heard him, Mattie. You and Janie Mae go on home and I'll catch up with you when I finish with old Eddie."

"Suits me," Mattie said, mocking the cocksure remark Virgil had made to Eddie a few minutes earlier. "Who wants to watch a couple of boys bloody each other's noses anyway?"

For the past few days she and Janie Mae and Virgil had walked home through the woods, and today she would just amble right on and enjoy her favorite part of the day while Eddie and Virgil did whatever they wanted to one another.

The morning passed with neither Virgil nor Eddie mentioning the proposed fight again. If word had gotten to Mrs. Gwen, she would have put a stop to all plans immediately. Fighting wasn't tolerated by any of the teachers.

By late morning when Mattie noticed Eddie stealing furtive glances at Virgil, she wondered if the fight would really take place.

Then the bell rang to end morning session, and Mattie went down the hall to Janie Mae's class, never looking back at Virgil, who headed out the side door.

Ordinarily when they planned to walk home, she was in no rush and allowed her sister to dawdle as long as she liked. But today she wanted only to be away from the school grounds quickly, to put as much distance as possible between herself and Virgil and Eddie.

Janie Mae couldn't find one of the drawings she had done that morning.

"It's all right," Mattie said. "We'll get it tomorrow."

Janie Mae looked up at her, her lip quivering.

"Okay," Mattie said, "I'll help you look." She had

enough on her mind today without trying, as Mother wished, to develop Janie Mae's tough skin.

Finally they found the drawing in a stack on the teacher's desk. Janie Mae grinned when she saw it.

"Oh, yeah," she said, "we put them there before snack time."

Mattie didn't often feel irritated with Janie Mae, but today she could have cheerfully swatted her. However, she knew that would just lead to another delay.

"Come on," she said. "Let's get going."

Janie Mae smiled and tucked her hand into Mattie's.

As they crossed the playground, Mattie saw three of Eddie's friends lounging near the swing area. She slowed down and looked at the boys. Well, she supposed they could be just hanging around wondering where Eddie had gone. She needed to get Janie Mae home. It was a nice day and maybe they'd play in the woods all afternoon. Maybe she'd even go down to the creek and sit on her rock.

The thought filled Mattie with a warm longing. Virgil was a big boy. He could take care of himself. Clearly, fighting was not girls' business anyway.

She tightened her grip on Janie Mae's hand and took a few more resolute steps. Then one of the boys moved away from the swing, casually sauntering toward the ball field. The other two followed.

"Hey," Mattie yelled. "Where do you think you're going?"

The boys stopped and looked at her in surprise.

"Where's Eddie?" she demanded.

This time they looked at one another.

"Well, uh, well . . . we don't know," one stammered.

"I bet he wants you to wait for him right here," she

said, and she and Janie Mae settled down on the swings.

"Naw, I think we'd better get on home," another boy said, edging toward the ball field.

Mattie looked at them scornfully. Obviously all their bravado was reflected from Eddie. Without him around, they weren't sure what to do.

"If anybody leaves here, I'm going straight to the principal's office and tell him he'd better go check the woods behind the ball field." She pushed her feet firmly against the earth, sending the swing high into the air. This wouldn't be such a bad way to spend part of the afternoon, she thought.

One of the boys bit his thumbnail, and they all shifted their weight from one foot to the other. They glanced from Mattie, calmly swinging, to the ball field, undisturbed in the early afternoon sun. Then suddenly one of them turned toward the woods, cupped his hands over his mouth, and blew, raising his fingers and pressing them back down as if he were playing an instrument.

The sound vaguely resembled the hoot of an owl, Mattie thought. It seemed to serve its purpose, for in just a few minutes Eddie ambled across the ball field, Virgil stalking behind him. Neither looked as if he'd been touched by the other.

As they approached the group near the swings, Virgil looked at Mattie. His red hair seemed to turn a shade brighter.

"What're you doing here?" he demanded. "I told you to go on home."

Mattie leaped from the swing. "Who do you think you're ordering around," she shouted. The nerve of him! She had just saved him from being ganged up on by Eddie's buddies, and this was her thanks.

One of Eddie's friends spoke before Virgil could reply. "Yeah, we had to stop her from going to the principal. That's why we warned you."

For an instant Mattie wished Daddy had taught *her* to box. She felt an awful urge to slam her fist right into the middle of the boy's face.

Eddie was rocking on his heels, his thumbs hooked through his belt loops. "Well, Virgil, I figured you'd find a way to hide behind a girl."

Virgil shifted his attention from Mattie. "Back there in the woods you didn't act so sure of yourself," he said. He looked at the three boys grouped behind Eddie. "I reckon there's more than one kind of hiding."

Now Eddie danced from one foot to the other. "Let's just settle this right now," he said.

Virgil turned his back to him and reached a hand toward Janie Mae, who sat pale and still on the swing watching all that was happening. "Come on," he said. "Let's go home. I ain't fighting on any school grounds."

As Mattie stooped to pick up Janie Mae's drawings, she saw Eddie lunge at Virgil. "Look out!" she shouted.

Virgil half turned at the sound of her voice, and the punch Eddie had aimed at his back fell on his left shoulder. Virgil staggered under the weight of the larger boy. Then Mattie saw his free right hand double into a fist and his arm begin its swing. The muscle at the edge of his shirtsleeve bulged against the fabric. She closed her eyes a split second before a dull thud and a grunt from Eddie told her the fight was under way.

Instantly she opened her eyes again. Virgil was hold-

ing his left arm near his face while he jabbed at Eddie
with his right. But fighting was second nature to Eddie,
and he was staying out of the way of most of Virgil's
blows. Only a large red spot on his jaw showed how
successful Virgil's first strike had been.

Mattie looked at Janie Mae. She seemed frozen to the
swing seat. What am I thinking, letting her watch this?
Mattie wondered. Quickly she went over to her, pulled
her off the seat, and hugged her tightly against her own
body. "Let's go home, Janie Mae," she whispered.

But Janie Mae shook her head. "They're going to
hurt Virgil," she cried.

"Virgil can take care of himself."

But Mattie wasn't so sure when she saw Eddie's
friends closing in on them. Was that why Eddie was
just dancing around and jabbing at Virgil? Was he expecting help?

Well, two can play that game, Mattie thought. She
dropped her arms from around Janie Mae and stepped
in front of the three boys. "If you want to fight, it's
going to have to be with me first," she said.

"Get outa here, Mattie," one of the boys said. "We
ain't got no quarrel with you."

"Seems to me you ain't got no quarrel with anybody.
This is supposed to be Eddie and Virgil's fight."

Another boy put a hand against her shoulder and
pushed. She dug her heels into the ground and didn't
move. He dropped his arm. "I'm not leaving until you
do," she said, staring straight at him.

Behind her she heard Eddie and Virgil shuffling their
feet on the packed playground soil. The dust they
stirred up rose like a cloud around the small group. The
dry, gritty taste reminded her of summer afternoon

drives along gravel mountain roads. But getting dusty on a ride wasn't bad because you were going where you wanted. Here it was a different story. She wasn't certain where this fight was going to take her, but she was pretty sure it wouldn't be to a place where she wanted to go.

Then, above the heavy breathing, she heard a voice.

"What's going on here?" It was Mr. Henderson, the principal.

The three boys facing her took a few steps back.

"Hold it right there. I don't want anybody leaving."

Mattie turned to see Eddie and Virgil standing on the dusty spot where they'd circled one another. Eddie's cockiness had evaporated, but Virgil still looked as if he'd like to take a swing at his tormentor. She wished she could warn him to look a little sorry so the principal wouldn't be too harsh.

"Were you involved in this fight?" Mr. Henderson asked, looking at her first.

She lowered her gaze. If by involved, he meant hitting someone, then she wasn't. But if he meant only wanting to hit someone, then she supposed she was as guilty as anyone.

But he took her quietness for denial and turned his attention to the boys. Eddie's three friends vigorously denied any part in the fight.

"Naw, we were just on our way home," one said. The other two nodded in unison, looking as if an off-stage hand were controlling both their heads by pulling one string.

Mr. Henderson looked at Janie Mae. "I'm sure she had nothing to do with this. Take her along home," he said to Mattie. Then he turned to Eddie and Virgil.

"Guess it'll just be the three of us going back to the office. Eddie, we've been through this before. And Virgil, is it? I remember your entering school a few months ago."

He walked back to the school building, Eddie and Virgil following him. But Virgil still didn't look contrite, Mattie noticed. However, she decided, there wasn't anything she could do to help him now.

She took Janie Mae's hand and started for home. Eddie's three friends had slunk away as soon as Mr. Henderson turned his back. Now she and Janie Mae trudged across the playground.

"What's going to happen to Virgil?" Janie Mae asked. "Will the principal paddle him?"

Mattie shook her head. She didn't know what punishment Mr. Henderson might mete out, but she had a feeling it wouldn't be nearly as bad as what Virgil would face at home.

Mother reacted just as Mattie thought she would. She took one look at their faces when they arrived home without Virgil, then motioned for them to sit at the table with her.

"Where is he?" she asked.

"There was a little trouble," Mattie said.

"Fighting?"

Mattie nodded.

Mother clenched her jaw.

Half an hour later Virgil arrived, looking even more angry than he had when he faced Eddie. Mother dried her hands on her apron and sat down once more at the kitchen table. "All right, Virgil," she said, "tell me what happened."

Virgil dug at the floor with the toe of his shoe, the

squeak of rubber against hardwood causing Mattie to cringe.

"It was just Eddie. He wanted to fight today."

"And you had to oblige him?"

"There wasn't no way around it, unless I wanted to be called yellow all my life."

Mother rubbed her forehead with her fingertips. "Well, at least you don't look any the worse for it."

"No, Mr. Henderson broke it up before we hardly got started."

"Mr. Henderson? Surely you weren't fighting on school grounds."

Virgil nodded mutely, but he glanced toward Mattie and clenched his jaw.

"Well, maybe being called up before the principal has put a stop to this fighting business."

"Yes'm, I reckon it has."

At Virgil's tone, Mother looked up. "Is there something else you aren't telling me?" she asked.

Once more Virgil nodded.

Mother sighed. "All right, let's have it."

"Well, I won't be going to school for a few days."

Mother didn't look as surprised as Mattie felt.

"How long are you suspended for?" Mother asked.

"Three days. Me and Eddie both." Now Virgil dug even harder at the floor with his toe. "And . . . and after the three days, you or Uncle Omer will have to go back with me to talk to Mr. Henderson."

Mother rose and pushed her chair away from the table. "Well, for the three days I'll find plenty for you to do around here. We might as well work off some of that energy you want to spend in fighting."

"Yes, ma'am," Virgil said. Then he left the room.

Mattie followed him. He glared at her. "I reckon you know this is your fault."

Mattie just looked at him. First he'd made Daddy an FBI man. Now he blamed her for the fact that neither he nor Eddie had good sense. Well, if anyone was suffering a shortage of crazy cousins, she knew where there was a spare one.

13

DURING VIRGIL'S THREE-DAY SUSPENSION, Mother kept him at work hauling wheelbarrow loads of loamy soil from the woods to an area where sunlight penetrated the tall oaks and where she was determined to grow the pretty cosmos that had surrounded their Kentucky home. Each day when Mattie came home she heard the rattle of the metal wheelbarrow wheel across the stones of the lawn. She figured Mother and Virgil had their work cut out for them if they planned to redo that lawn.

She watched Virgil pushing the heaped wheelbarrow. In the heat he had shed his shirt, and the muscles above his shoulder blades rippled as he maneuvered the load. Boy, she said to herself, if Jesse could see you, he'd sure want you to come live with him and be "right handy around the place." But there'd been no word from the man, and Virgil had stopped checking the mail every day.

Virgil didn't say anything more to Mattie about his troubles being her fault. As a matter of fact, he hardly spoke to her at all. If she started to tell him something that had happened at school, he just hurried past her as if moving dirt were the most important thing on earth. His silence seemed to be reserved primarily for her. Even Mother, who was inflicting the punishment, was spoken to in a civil manner. And Daddy and Janie Mae were treated to his comments on the day's happenings.

One evening, as Mattie sat reading a book on their small porch, she overheard part of a conversation between Mother and Daddy.

"I don't care if I am working him too hard," Mother said. "Virgil may not learn to hate fighting, but he'll learn that one of the consequences of fighting isn't very pleasant. And I don't care if Eddie is a bully. There's got to be a better way of dealing with bullies than trying to knock them flat. Look at the shape that kind of thinking has left the world in."

Mattie didn't know whether or not it was due to bullies, but from what she heard on the radio and saw in the newsreels, the world was in bad shape. Even though Germany had surrendered on May 7, ending the war in Europe, out in the Pacific Ocean thousands and thousands of young Americans were fighting to capture the island of Okinawa from the Japanese. Mattie realized that Jimmy Dale might be sent there someday, since he was due to graduate in a few more days and planned to go straight into the service. Each time she went to the movies, the newsreels showed the goggled and helmeted figures of Japanese pilots diving in their planes. Janie Mae's terror returned often, and Mattie could only rub her sister's back and whisper meaningless words of comfort.

Maybe Mother was right about the consequences of fighting. At any rate, when Virgil's three-day suspension was over, Mother and Daddy both returned to school with him. Mattie and Janie Mae rode along in the car, but they headed down the hallway to their classrooms while the adults and Virgil went in the opposite direction toward the principal's office. The last Mattie saw of Virgil, he was shifting nervously from foot to foot, his red hair standing straight up where he'd run his hands through it.

The cowlick was still in disarray when he entered the classroom half an hour later. Everyone looked up, and a few of the boys silently gripped their hands together and half raised them in a salute to his success with Eddie. Virgil was the first who had battled Eddie and not been badly beaten in the fracas. And no one counted it as a draw just because Eddie was not battle-scarred either.

With someone like Eddie, Mattie thought, you have to count whatever you can as a victory. Now that Virgil was back in class, she felt a little proud of him, too.

Mrs. Gwen seemed to be the only one who didn't appreciate what Virgil had accomplished.

"We're glad to have you back," she said, when he entered the classroom. "But I trust we won't have a recurrence of Monday's scene, no matter what the provocation."

Virgil nodded.

"I'll take the assignments you completed at home." She held out her hand and Virgil placed in it the arithmetic and spelling lessons he'd worked on each evening when his outdoor chores were done.

Eddie came in an hour later, and he and Virgil studiously ignored one another for the rest of the day. As a matter of fact, Mattie felt that she and Eddie and his group were all getting the same treatment from Virgil.

She wondered what she had done to put herself in league with them.

She found out on the way home.

Virgil walked along through the woods, kicking at clumps of sodden leaves, exposing the white net-veining on the green foliage of rattlesnake plantain, stirring up the aroma of earth ready for growth. He spoke mostly to Janie Mae. But finally, as if something inside him threatened to burst, he turned to Mattie.

"Why'd you do it?" he asked.

Mattie looked around. What had she done?

"Why were you going to tell the principal?"

"Oh, come on, Virgil. Surely you didn't believe Eddie's friends."

"But you were there on the playground when you were supposed to go home. You're the one who got me in trouble."

"So that's how it is." Mattie put her chin in the air and lengthened her stride. "If you're that bullheaded, you just believe whatever you want."

Virgil lengthened his stride to keep up with her. Janie Mae straggled behind.

"Anyway, I reckon everything worked out. It didn't hurt me much to do all that work for Aunt Lucy, and she didn't send me back to Kentucky." He smiled magnanimously at Mattie. "I reckon I forgive you."

Mattie stopped and stared at him. "What do you mean, you forgive me? I didn't ask you to, and I won't let you. You can't forgive somebody who hasn't done anything wrong.

"And it's a good thing," she added, "I don't believe in fighting or I'd be sorely tempted, Virgil, to pound some sense into you."

Virgil laughed. "I reckon I'd have to let you. I don't hold with hitting girls."

Mattie turned on her heel and stomped home through the woods. Janie Mae had caught up, and Virgil walked along beside her, whistling through his teeth.

Daddy arrived home from work that evening with a message from Fred. As soon as Mattie and Virgil were out of school, she wanted them to spend a week with her to help her put up the hay.

"She can't pay you," Daddy said. "But she said there'd be time to fish and swim and hunt. And she'd even cook a fresh meal every day." He laughed, but Mother just raised her eyebrows.

The final week of school always seemed long, and this year Mattie found it almost unbearable. She thought constantly of the river and of the days she would spend wandering around Fred's farm, watching the animals and doing as she pleased. And she was looking forward to seeing Fred again. Below Fred's gruff ways, Mattie had seen a core of gentleness when she spoke about her animals. As for the chores Mattie and Virgil were supposed to help with, Mattie didn't know anything about putting up hay, but she figured it couldn't be all that hard.

She soon found out she wasn't completely right about hay. The weather hit one of its scorching periods the day Daddy delivered her and Virgil to Fred's farm. "Don't work too hard," Daddy said with a laugh, as he drove away from the farm, dust boiling up behind the car so that a cloud of it remained long after he was out of sight.

Fred fanned her face with her hand. "Whew," she

said, "let's get in out of this dust and heat."

As they crossed the cool darkness of the living room. Mattie noticed that the piano still bore its burden of plants and pictures. Nothing in the room appeared to have been disturbed since their last visit. Not even the dust. Boy, she thought, wouldn't Gran have a good time cleaning here.

Fred might not share Gran's enthusiasm for getting rid of dirt, but Mattie detected a similarity in the two women in the way Fred looked her over while they stood in the kitchen drinking the cold spring water.

"You look strong enough to be a good hand in the field," she said approvingly.

Mattie figured she was right. She'd always been able to do whatever work came her way, except, of course, for splitting that stubborn kindling wood.

Fred didn't comment on Virgil's potential for doing the work. Mattie guessed even Fred took for granted that boys were naturally strong physically.

"Well, let's get on with it then." And Fred strode to the back door. Mattie and Virgil followed her. "You'll need these." She handed each of them a large-brimmed straw hat, and pushed a third one down on her own head. "That sun can get pretty bad, even this early in the summer."

The hat smelled of dry summer fields, and the leather band inside it was rippled with discoloration from many perspiring heads. Mattie put it on, but it made her hair feel itchy, so she let it fall onto her back, the string that served as a chin strap preventing her from losing it.

"I started cutting a few days ago when I got word you two'd be here today. I sure was relieved. Near killed myself last summer. No help to be had with all the men at war. Now we got a field all ready to be put up," Fred said, as she led them into the barn where two large horses hung their heads over the doors to the stalls. "We'll just harness Bill here to the rake and Joe to the wagon, and then we'll be all set."

Fred moved easily about the barn, leading the two enormous horses as if they were small children, rigging a harness on one and then the other. Her fingers were as deft with the leather straps as Mother's were with needle and thread. In the barnyard she attached Bill's rigging to a rake with curved teeth that arched like pictures Mattie had seen of ocean waves ready to break. A metal seat was perched forward of the teeth, and a lever next to the seat raised and lowered the teeth. The wagon Fred hitched Joe to looked harmless in comparison.

When Fred had finished, she took the horses' reins and led them to the field. Mattie realized from the slack in the reins that the horses knew where they were going without any directing.

The heat they'd escaped in the house and barn waited for them in the hay field. The closely dropped grass exposed earth that soaked up the sun's rays and seemed to return them tenfold to Mattie's feet and legs. There was no spring smell of earth in the field, only the dry, nose-tingling sensation of sunbaked grass and dust. The feeling that she was going to burst into a fit of sneezing any moment seized Mattie as she bent to her task.

She and Virgil shared the job of picking up the cut hay as Bill and Fred raked it. Fred sat on the metal seat atop the rake. Mattie marveled at Fred's grace as she held the reins in one hand and with the other worked the lever. As the rake teeth gathered the hay into a pile, Fred pulled the lever, lifting the teeth and leaving a haystack for Mattie and Virgil to toss onto the wagon, which Joe docilely pulled alongside. The big brown horse obviously knew the routine, for he needed no hand on the reins that lay idle across his back. He stopped at each pile of hay and waited patiently while Mattie and Virgil pitchforked it onto the wagon.

"Better pile it in the middle first," Fred warned, pointing to the wagon, "else we won't get much on the wagon and we'll make too many trips to the barn."

Mattie was perspiring by the time they'd loaded one stack. Already Fred and Bill were turning the first corner, and another dry-looking mass of hay was waiting halfway down the field. Mattie had put the hat back on her head after about five minutes, its itchiness no great discomfort compared with the dizzying effect of the sun on her scalp. Virgil didn't seem to be having any easier time of it.

They were still working on the second haystack when Fred pulled Bill into the shade, hopped down from the seat, and came toward them. "Guess old Bill needs a little cooling. Pulling that rake is hard work. And he's cantankerous, so I can't trust him to follow along like Joe here." She gave Joe an affectionate pat. "Let me give you two a hand." Mattie noticed that the heat didn't seem to bother Fred in spite of her large size.

With Fred's help the rest of the stack was quickly placed on the wagon. Then Fred returned to Bill, and Mattie and Virgil followed Joe to the next haystack. An hour later, with the wagon heaped so high that the last forkful of hay barely fit, Fred once more left Bill and the rake in the shade and joined Mattie and Virgil.

"Okay, Joe," she said, "let's get to the barn."

Without anyone to lead him, Joe plodded back up the hill. "No need for you young-uns to walk," Fred said. "Just climb up on the wagon."

Mattie leaped onto the back of the wagon and settled gratefully against the hay, her feet dangling over the wagon's edge. Virgil jumped onto the other side. Fred continued to walk, keeping time with Joe. Mattie wondered if the woman walked because she was used to it or if she just didn't feel it was fair to give Joe more to pull than he already had.

Loading the hay into the barn was even more work than putting it onto the wagon had been. Fred stood on top of the load and pitchforked the hay into the barn loft. Mattie and Virgil relayed the forkfuls into a corner of the cavernous loft.

"Get it plumb back in the corners," Fred cautioned with the first forkful. "This barn has to hold a whole summer of hay."

Mattie looked at the space to be filled. The roof towered over her head, vaulting toward the sky like the steeples of churches she'd seen in movies. The first load of hay huddled in a corner. What had seemed a large amount on the wagon was now reduced to meaningless forkfuls flung far back in the hayloft. She and Virgil and Fred had worked more than an hour to put that small mound of hay into the barn. And Fred and the horses had worked several days cutting the field. How many hours of work would be required to fill the barn loft to the roof? To Mattie the task looked as impossible as building a pyramid must have looked to the Egyptian slaves.

14

MATTIE WAS FILLED WITH THANKS AS SHE SAW the sun sink behind the Cumberlands. She knew only darkness would stop Fred and Bill and Joe, who looked as if they could work steadily all night if someone provided them with light.

Fred walked briskly back to the house, Mattie and Virgil trailing behind her. Fred slapped her hat against her leg, bits of hay flying into the air, and said in her usual booming voice, "Well, now, tomorrow morning soon as the sun dries off the dew, we'll finish up that last field. Then I reckon you young-uns can have the afternoon off while me and the horses cut a couple more fields."

Mattie sighed. If she just lived long enough to finish up that field, she'd be more than happy to have the afternoon off. She'd stretch out in the clear river and let her body return to something that felt as if it belonged to a human.

Fred lit a lantern and set it on the kitchen table. Then she removed a few bowls from the icebox and ladled up potato salad, pickled beans, and coleslaw onto the plates. "I told Lucy I'd feed you young-uns, and I aim to keep my word." She looked at Mattie, who sat with her head cradled in her arms on the table. "Buck up, now. A few vittles'll be just the ticket."

Mattie was sure her jaws wouldn't work, but when the first forkful of food slid between her teeth, she perked up. Fred might not be an excellent cook, but she made good potato salad, and the coldness of the food was in itself a comfort.

Mattie fell asleep on a black iron bed in the back bedroom. Obviously the room wasn't used regularly, but Fred had dusted the heavy furniture and had covered the bed with a fresh quilt still smelling of sunshine. After the hours of work, Mattie felt she could have slept anywhere, but she nevertheless enjoyed for a few moments before falling asleep the solitude of having the big bed all to herself.

She awoke with the sun streaming through the windows. The aroma of coffee and bacon was as strong in the room as was the light. She leaped from bed, but when she raised her arms to put on a shirt, she thought about lying down again. Her arms felt as if she'd been picking up elephants. And I guess, she thought, that's about what I did yesterday.

Virgil and Fred were at the table when Mattie entered the kitchen.

"Morning, morning," Fred boomed.

Virgil just grinned and went on eating. Mattie wondered if his muscles were as sore as hers, but she wasn't going to ask and have him tell her only girls got aching muscles from putting up hay.

After breakfast, while Fred finished the morning chores, Mattie walked down to the river. She sniffed deeply as she passed the cornfield, though she knew it

was too early in the season for corn to be tasseled out.
But she smelled the first honeysuckle blooms along the
fencerows and the freshness of the June morning.
When she reached the river, she stood beside it, idly
throwing stones across a pool formed where rocks
dammed the flow of water. Her arm hurt a little less
with each motion, and she was concentrating on the
loosening of her muscles when Virgil walked up.

"Want me to show you how to skip stones?"

She nearly blurted no, but he was already looking
around for a suitable stone.

"Okay," she said.

Virgil drew his arm back in a sideways motion. The
stone slapped the water, then arched above it, touched
down once more and rose again. On the third contact
it sank beneath the surface.

"Shoot," he said, "just two hops."

He hadn't even flinched. His muscles must be all
right.

"What you gotta do is hold the rock like this." He
picked up another smooth stone and wrapped his
thumb and index finger around it.

But Mattie had found out what she wanted to know.
Maybe those three days of pushing the wheelbarrow
for Mother had paid off in more ways than Virgil knew.

"We'd better go see if Fred's ready for us," she said.

Virgil skipped the stone, making this one hop three
times. Then he followed her up the hill.

"I brought my gun," he said, as he caught up with
her.

He didn't need to remind her. Mother had been hor-
rified when he'd taken the gun from the closet. Daddy

had calmed her as best he could and then had gone to Town Hall to register it. "Just so we'll be legal," he had said.

Virgil looked around at the meadows of green grass and clover and the fencerows with their protective covering. "This here farm is a good place for rabbits, and I been thinking I'd like to get one for Fred," he said. "Wanta go hunting with me early tomorrow morning?"

"Ugh," Mattie said. "You mean go out and shoot a little rabbit like you did that day in the woods?"

"Yeah, sure. That's what people do when they go hunting."

"Not me."

"Okay, just thought I'd ask."

Fred had the horses ready again when Mattie and Virgil reached the barn. The sun was as hot as it had been the day before, and Mattie put on the hat right away. After a few minutes of lifting the loads of hay, she was moving with an easy rhythm, the soreness of her muscles forgotten. They put the last wagon load in the barn just at lunchtime.

When they reached the house, Fred took the potato salad, pickled beans, and coleslaw once more from the refrigerator. Again, the food was cold and refreshing, but Mattie began to wonder if this was going to be the menu for the whole week. Maybe Virgil's hunting trip wasn't such a bad idea.

"Me and Bill and Joe'll be cutting hay all afternoon," Fred said, after they had eaten. "You young-uns just do what you want."

Mattie was glad to hear that. The one thing she

wanted to do was sink into the river and not even think about hay and dry, hot fields.

"But I reckon it wouldn't be a good idea to go swimming all by yourself. Better buddy up if you wanta get wet." Fred laughed, causing the dogs who were lying on the back porch, noses as near the kitchen as was allowed, to raise their heads. "Me and the horses'll be getting wet right out in the sun."

"I don't much like to swim," Virgil said, when Mattie suggested their afternoon activity.

Uh-oh, she thought, here it comes. Now I'm going to have to go hunting after all.

But Virgil didn't have that in mind. "Tell you what, I'll come down to the river and fish or skip rocks while you swim."

And he did. He sat on the bank and dangled a line into the water. But he didn't catch any fish. "Don't reckon it's the right time of day," he said. Still, he looked happy.

Mattie was happy, too. Floating on the water, kicking occasionally, looking up at the blue sky, feeling every muscle in her body relax—she couldn't think of any better way to spend an afternoon.

Finally she climbed out of the water and lay across a rock, letting the sun dry her. Funny, she thought, how good the sun feels here at the river and how awful it was up in the hay fields.

Virgil rolled up his fishing line.

Mattie sighed. Fair is fair, she thought. "Okay, Virgil," she said, "I'll go hunting with you tomorrow."

He nodded. "We'll go just before sunrise," he said. "That's the best time to hunt."

Next morning the back bedroom was still dark when Mattie heard Virgil tap on the door. She pulled on blue jeans and a shirt, her toes curling against the cold lino-leum floor.

They stepped out into a quiet world of gray. Trees and sky were indistinguishable, and Mattie wondered how they would find any animals. Again the world smelled of honeysuckle and early morning, a smell that belonged to the country and to summer.

Virgil led the way across the pasture and into an area of woods that sloped down to the river. He motioned to a fallen log. "We'll just wait till the rabbits come out to feed," he said, settling onto the log, his gun across his knees.

Mattie sat down, too. Now the eastern sky was growing lighter and she could see in the nearby pasture blades of grass tipped with dew. The darker foliage of clover nestled in clumps throughout the grass. As her eyes adjusted, she saw a movement to her right. Then a brownish form hopped into view. Virgil's hand slowly descended to his gun. Mattie wanted to scream at the rabbit, but she sat motionless. The rabbit raised its head, nose twitching rapidly. Then it laid its ears flat against its head and, with several bounding leaps, was gone.

"Gol-ol-lee," Virgil breathed. "That was a big one." He stood up. "Reckon we're upwind from him."

They walked along the edge of the woods to a place where the line of trees curved back into the field. There they sat beneath a large oak, the eastern sky at their backs. They sat without talking for about a quarter of an hour, and Mattie was just beginning to think that hunting wasn't so bad after all, when another rabbit hopped into view. This one was smaller than the earlier one, but it was the same brownish-gray color and its tail showed a white cottony underside each time it hopped.

Again Virgil dropped his hand to his gun. Again the rabbit busily twitched its nose. However, it hopped closer to Mattie and Virgil. Then it began nibbling on the clover leaves.

Virgil had the gun against his shoulder. He laid his cheek along the stock, squinted his eyes, and leveled the rifle barrel. With his thumb he cocked the hammer. Mattie felt as if she were watching a film in slow motion. The rabbit hopped to another clump of clover. Virgil shifted the gun barrel. Slowly his index finger drew back the trigger, and an explosion ripped through the air. The rabbit's body gave one convulsive leap and fell over. Mattie thought of Janie Mae's horror when the other rabbit had been killed, and she shared those feelings now. She knew Virgil was using a real gun and that he had come to the field intending to kill a rabbit. But she had come along willingly. She might as well have pulled the trigger herself.

Virgil walked to the rabbit, picked it up by the back feet, and held it at arm's length. "A young buck," he said. "He'll make fine stew, and nobody'll miss him."

"What do you mean—nobody'll miss him?" Mattie shouted into the stillness.

The death of the rabbit was suddenly as real to her as any death she knew—as real as Opal lying in the casket in the heavily scented church, as real as President Roosevelt lying in state in a flag-draped casket, more real than the thousands of figures of war dead she heard recited on the news.

"How do you know nobody will miss him? Maybe he had brothers and sisters he played with in the pasture each evening. Don't you think they'll wonder where he is? Won't they miss something in their games, a familiar back they used to leap over?"

"What're you so mad about?" Virgil asked, as he walked toward her, the rabbit dangling from his hand.

"I'm not mad. I'm just disgusted that you can kill something and not even care."

"Mattie, it's a rabbit, for Pete's sake. Everybody kills them and eats them."

Virgil walked a few steps closer. "You used to eat rabbit stew all the time in Kentucky. What's the matter with you?"

Mattie looked at the rabbit. It was as if it had never been alive, had not been eating clover in the summer sun a few minutes earlier. Where had the part of it that counted gone? Or was all that mattered right there, dangling from Virgil's hand, a carcass to be put in a pot and fed to a few hungry people? Where did what mattered about humans go when they died? If a human death was a terrible thing, how could she be sure an animal death wasn't also?

"I guess I used to do a lot of dumb things. But that doesn't mean I have to go on doing them." She turned and ran back through the woods and across the pasture, leaving Virgil with his gun on one shoulder and the dead rabbit in his hand.

15

✻ ♪✻♪✻♪✻♪✻

BY THE TIME DADDY RETURNED FOR THEM,
Mattie and Virgil were as brown as they usually were
late in the summer. Mattie was able to work right along
with Virgil and keep up with him. They had half filled
the barn loft with hay—a feat Mattie had thought impossible a week earlier. And they had eaten all the
potato salad and pickled beans. Virgil and Fred had
eaten the rabbit stew, but Mattie had refused to touch
it. Virgil had given her a puzzled look the first time she
refused it. After that, he had shrugged his shoulders
and eaten two helpings.

"Now you young-uns come on back anytime and
enjoy the farm," Fred boomed, as they climbed into the
car. "It ain't always just work out here." Then she
laughed and slapped her thigh. Mattie knew Fred
would head for the cornfield as soon as she could harness Joe to the cultivator. She'd fretted the past two
days about weeds shading out the tender young plants.
Not all work indeed!

Daddy was quiet on the drive home. Mattie wondered if he had been working too hard. Lately he had
put in long hours of overtime. It was as if V-E Day, the
cessation of war in Europe, hadn't occurred. If what

Daddy did at that well-guarded plant had anything to do with the fighting, then why hadn't things slowed down?

But his quietness had nothing to do with overwork. "Virgil," he said finally, as they drove along the Oak Ridge Turnpike, "we got a letter from home. Your dad, Jesse, has appeared from nowhere. He's demanding you come live with him."

Virgil looked out the window as if he were patiently waiting for a rabbit.

"It looks like the law is on his side. I'm sorry, son, but I'm going to have to take you back to Kentucky tomorrow."

Son. Mattie was stunned by the word, as stunned by its sound on her father's lips as she was by his news.

It had never occurred to her that he might have always wanted a son, someone he could teach to box, someone he could go hunting with.

They rode the rest of the way in silence. Mattie knew Daddy and Virgil were thinking of the next day. She could think only of that hateful word she had just heard.

Before going to bed that night, Virgil sat on the sofa and cleaned his gun.

"Guess you'll have more chances to use that now," Daddy said, to break the silence that enveloped all of them.

Virgil nodded.

Mattie watched him pull the bit of oiled cloth out of the barrel of the gun. She thought about both times she had seen him use the gun, the first resulting in a useless death, a rabbit to be hidden, the second in a pot of stew he and Fred had enjoyed for two days. Maybe there were some things he would like about being back in Kentucky—hunting anytime he wanted, for example. But she wasn't sure even hunting was going to make up for everything else, especially for Jesse. She remembered the expression on Virgil's face that night before Opal's funeral when Jesse had appeared, the way he had guarded the secret of that appearance, and his furtive searches of the mail.

Next morning Mattie awoke to a quiet house. Daddy and Virgil had left before sunup. Because they used the car as little as possible between trips to Kentucky, Daddy had plenty of gas coupons to get there and back.

She slipped from bed and went into the living room. Virgil's sheet and blanket were still crumpled on the sofa. Well, she thought, I've waited nearly four months for this day. I ought to be skipping about the house, flinging open the windows, shouting to the world that pesky Virgil has finally gone.

Instead she folded the bedding and plumped up the sofa cushions. Then she went out onto the porch, sat on the top step, leaning her back against the coolness of the house, and waited to be happy.

Through the remainder of June and all of July, with Virgil gone, she had moments of being contented. Most mornings she took Janie Mae to the recreational program at the school playground. Sometimes her own friends were there, just hanging around watching the younger children and remembering how it was to go to school at Highland View, as if it had all happened some time in the remote past. The only reality for them seemed to be junior high coming up in the fall. A new school, a junior high, would open to ease overcrowding in the elementary schools. No longer would the older students have to share facilities with the earlier grades.

After a few weeks, Robert started showing up at the playground whenever she was there.

"You know why he's here," one of her friends whispered one day.

Mattie shook her head.

"We mentioned that you always brought Janie Mae, and next day he was right here, like the playground was the most interesting place on earth."

"Well, maybe he just got bored being at home."

"Sure he did," she said with a laugh.

One morning while Janie Mae was listening to story hour, Robert sat down on the swing next to the one where Mattie idly pushed herself back and forth. She noticed he seemed to have grown a few more inches during the summer. His face had matured also, with the jawline firm and almost square above shoulders that had broadened.

"Haven't seen Virgil all summer," he said.

"He had to go back to Kentucky." Mattie was sure Robert knew where Virgil was. She and her friends had discussed his leaving several times. But maybe Robert was just making conversation—the aimless kind, to pass the day, the way grown-ups so often did.

"The softball team could use him. You ought to come out and watch us some evening. We've got a good team. Tom's on it. Even old Eddie's been coming out and playing."

Mattie nodded. She'd thought about playing on the girls' team, but Mother wouldn't let her go to the playground in the evenings. Besides, she was content to spend her evenings with her books, sitting on a quilt beneath the trees, watching night settle on the earth and feeling the day's heat lift.

"Reckon," Robert pushed his foot extra hard against the ground, causing his swing to lurch backward. "Reckon," he repeated when he had the swing moving smoothly again, "you could go to the movies with me Saturday afternoon?"

Mattie looked at him, her eyes opened wide. Was Robert asking her for a date? She knew she ought to feel flattered. Some of her friends talked almost constantly of what they'd do the first time a boy asked them out. But she'd never given it any thought. Now, all she felt was dismay. She thought of Robert's damp hand holding her hand through a movie, and she tried not to grimace. Not that she didn't like him. She just couldn't picture herself with a "boyfriend."

"I can't do that," she finally answered. "My mother wouldn't let me."

"Well, I'll see you around," Robert said. He jumped from the swing and ran to join a group of boys who were crossing the playground. Mattie sighed with relief. Maybe persistence was one thing Robert lacked— at least, she hoped so.

When Mattie and Janie Mae got home that afternoon, Mother was reading a letter from Gran.

"Well, I never," she said as she smoothed the lined tablet sheets. "I wouldn't have thought such even of Jesse."

"What's happened?" Mattie asked.

"We all knew that man was lazy and good for nothing, but you'd think a little of the milk of human kindness would run through his veins for his own son."

"What's he done?" Mattie asked again, trying not to let her impatience show.

"He tried to send Virgil into the mines."

"But Virgil's too young."

"Thank goodness for that. And thank goodness Sonny Jenkins knows everything that goes on in eastern Kentucky."

Mother told Mattie and Janie Mae the story. Jesse had hired Virgil out to do all sorts of odd jobs—spade up areas for late gardens, paint houses, build porches—anything that needed to be done. With so many men away at war, there were plenty of jobs to be had, jobs that needed more strength than skill. Virgil was making Jesse a pretty good living, it appeared to everybody.

But according to Gran, Jesse wasn't satisfied with just having enough. He kept looking at Virgil's back and arms growing stronger every day, and he kept thinking about the hourly wages being paid men to go underground and dig out the coal that the war effort burned so fast.

Mother picked up the letter and read Gran's words:

"Jesse took Virgil over the mountain into Hawkins County and passed him off for sixteen. Well, you'd think even a fool like Jesse would know Virgil don't look that old. The mine owner said Virgil could start in a week. Then he commenced asking around about the red-haired kid and his daddy. Word got to Sonny and he headed straight over the mountain. On Virgil's first day at work, Sonny was standing at the mine entrance. He warned Jesse that if he tried anything like that again, he'd be hauled up before a judge."

Mattie could picture most of the scene—Sonny with his gun strapped around his waist, Jesse shuffling his feet and looking from the corners of his eyes. But she couldn't see Virgil. How did he react? Did he stand with his feet apart and glare at the men? Or had the months with Jesse taught him to hang his head at any confrontation?

Mother folded the sheets and tucked them back into the envelope. "That's all Gran wrote except for her worries about Jimmy Dale."

"What's wrong with Jimmy Dale?" Janie Mae asked.

"Nothing's wrong with him. But he's in boot camp now, and everybody is worried he'll be sent to join the fighting in the Pacific."

Mattie remembered the recent newsreels of the war. U.S. forces had regained the Philippines and then had taken the island of Okinawa after nearly three months of fighting. The bombing attacks against Japanese cities had intensified throughout the summer. She shuddered. She knew the terror of Janie Mae's nightmares not only through her sister's disturbed sleep but also through the faces she saw in her own imagination. And soon Jimmy Dale might be over there in the middle of all of it.

But as terrible as that thought seemed, the reality of Virgil's plight seemed worse. How would it be to know your own father didn't care about you, that he valued you only for what you could earn for him?

She thought back to the day Daddy had called Virgil son. Maybe the word had just slipped from Daddy's lips. Neither he nor Virgil had made any note of it. They'd just fallen into silence. Maybe Virgil was Daddy's son in a sense of the word that had nothing to do with birth.

And no matter what the relationship was between them, did it lessen in any way the special bond that'd always been between her and Daddy?

"I guess that's what I've got to figure out," she said.

Mother looked startled. "You have to figure out if Jimmy Dale is going to be sent into the fighting?"

"No, no," Mattie said. "I was just thinking out loud."

At supper time Mattie set the table for the four of them. The arrangement was nice and tidy—a plate and a chair to each side of the table, no bunching up to squeeze in an extra person. And she and Janie Mae had more room now in their closet and in their chest of drawers—not that Virgil's few belongings had taken much space. She wondered where Virgil and Jesse were living. Gran hadn't said. Probably in a one-room shack up a hollow. Someplace where Jesse wouldn't have to pay rent.

"Mattie!" Mother said.

Mattie jumped, almost dropping the salt and pepper shakers.

"You must have been a million miles away. Look what you've done."

Mattie looked at the table. There lay the silverplate with its worn spots showing dark metal, the eating utensils she'd handled daily since she was old enough to feed herself. But the table looked strange—she had placed all the forks beside one plate, the spoons beside another, the knives beside the third, and the napkins near the fourth.

Mother laughed. "You've been absentminded all afternoon. Now you've spilled salt, and you know what that's supposed to mean. Better throw some over your left shoulder."

Mattie sprinkled a few grains on her palm and tossed them over her shoulder. That should guard against bad luck.

But, she thought, sometimes it's awful hard to tell good luck from bad.

16

ON THE FIRST MONDAY MORNING IN AUGUST
Mattie stood in the small living room ironing the
clothes Mother earlier had dampened and rolled tightly
in a basket. As she moved the iron back and forth,
steam rose, causing the hair she'd pushed away from
her face to curl against her cheeks. But she didn't mind.
Ironing was one of her favorite chores. She liked to
smell the fresh aroma of sunshine released from the
clothes by the heat of the iron. She liked to watch the
wrinkled fabric grow smooth as the iron passed over it.
There was an orderliness to the whole process that
pleased her.

While she ironed, she listened to the radio. Suddenly
a crackle of static interrupted the music, and a voice
broke in. Mattie caught only the words *Harry S Truman.*

Surely nothing had happened to the new president
too. She reached over and adjusted the dial. Then the
voice became clear.

"Mother, there's something on the radio about the
president," she shouted.

Mother came in from the porch where she'd been
snapping beans Daddy had brought home from Fred's.
Mother stood close to the radio. The newscaster con-

tinued, " . . . dropped a bomb on Hiroshima. It is an atomic bomb."

"What's an atomic bomb?" Mattie asked.

Mother shook her head and placed a finger against her lips as she leaned nearer the radio.

". . . our hope that Japan will now surrender and the war will be ended."

"Is it possible?" Mattie asked. "Could the war be almost over?"

"We can all hope so, if Truman says it. He's not one to make idle promises."

For the remainder of the day neighbors ran in and out and everyone stayed tuned to a radio station. As the plant workers returned home, they brought additional news.

"We did it."

"We were part of it."

"Maybe we've helped end the worst war in history."

Daddy tried to explain the news to Mattie and Janie Mae. "This whole town was set up just to build the atomic bomb. We've all been working on it, but none of us had any idea that was what was going on. No wonder everything was kept so secret!" He paced around the room. "Then at work today an announcement came over the public address system. It said that we had produced the critical parts of the bomb and that we could all be proud of our part in ending the war."

Mother nodded. "I guess that explains a lot of the secrecy, the awful search through luggage and inspection of every car in and out of Oak Ridge." She looked troubled, as Mattie had noticed she had looked from time to time all day. "It sounds like such a powerful weapon. Such a lot of people killed. Makes you wonder if anything could be worth that. But the president feels sure it will end the war, so maybe lives will be saved. Still . . ."

But all the wishes that Japan would immediately surrender were in vain. Three days later the family listened to announcements of the dropping of another bomb, this one on Nagasaki. The number of deaths from the first bomb were still being estimated, but the devastation was so complete that everyone wondered how the Japanese leaders could ignore the suffering of the people and continue to fight. Mother again shook her head over the announcements.

Finally the surrender came.

Mother closed her eyes for a few moments when she heard the news. "That means no more American soldiers will be sent off to fight. It means Jimmy Dale is safe."

"It means," Mattie said, "that Janie Mae's nightmares can stop. It means we can go to the movies without seeing newsreels of planes and tanks and ships."

Mother nodded. "Maybe it means no more killing, that everybody's sons are safe now."

That word again.

"Mother, was Daddy sad that Janie Mae and me were both girls?"

"Sad? Why, Mattie, what a strange thing to ask. Why would he have been sad?"

"Well, it seems as if everybody thinks boys are important. I just thought maybe he always wanted a son." The word came out hard, but at least it was out.

Mother cocked her head. "I don't guess Daddy or I ever thought about sons or daughters. We just wanted children—and we both were happy when you two were born perfectly healthy, pink and rosy as babies should be." She smiled.

But Mattie wasn't quite satisfied. "But how about later? Didn't he wish we'd play with cars and trucks and guns and things like that?"

Mother looked closely at her. "Mattie, are you just dreaming up trouble for yourself? Don't you remember how Daddy always came to your tea parties? He'd sit on the floor and hold your toy cups and have as good a time as you had.

"No, as far as I know he never missed the cars and trucks and guns." She laughed. "He probably had plenty of that kind of play with his own brothers when he was young."

Mattie sighed. Mother made everything sound so simple.

With Japan's surrender official, Oak Ridge celebrated. A big party was held in the main shopping area, and people danced on the nearby tennis courts. The McDowells went, along with their neighbors and everyone who didn't have to work that evening. Mattie was doubly glad for the celebration—glad the war was over and glad for a break in what was turning out to be a long summer.

She thought that Virgil would have enjoyed the party. He probably would have strutted around and bragged about how the *men* had won the war.

Many of her friends were at the celebration. When Robert saw her, he asked her to dance.

"I have to watch Janie Mae," she told him quickly. Well, he was persistent after all, she thought. And he was getting better-looking each time she saw him. Still, he was just another boy—probably as irritating to those who knew him well as Virgil was to her.

But even though Mattie wouldn't dance with him, she and Robert didn't escape the attention of some of their friends.

"Well, there you two are together," one of them said.

Mattie smiled, but she wanted to glare. She hurriedly changed the subject. "Aren't you glad school will be starting soon?" she asked.

The talk turned to what junior high would be like. "I'll never find my way around that big building," one girl said.

"And we'll probably all be split up in different classes and won't ever see each other," another said.

"Maybe you and Robert will get lucky and be in the same class."

Robert looked as uncomfortable as Mattie felt. "Yeah," he said, "well, I gotta be going. See you around."

"Wasn't that cute? I think he was blushing."

"Speaking of cute, is Virgil coming back when school starts?"

Mattie blinked. Did those girls actually think Virgil was cute? Virgil, with his thatch of red hair, his dare-the-world way of standing, and his conviction that boys were superior to girls?

Virgil seemed to be on everyone's mind. On the ride home Mother mentioned him, too. "It's just a few days till Virgil's birthday. I wonder where he is and what Jesse has him doing."

As if in answer to her question, a letter from Gran arrived the next day. Mattie and Janie Mae and Daddy sat around the table while Mother read it aloud.

"Virgil is back with me. Last week Jesse took the money Virgil had made and lit out. Virgil stayed on in the place where they were living, thinking Jesse would come back, but after a few days he gave up and walked around here to our house. Truth is, I think Virgil was scared to leave Jesse. He won't tell me right out, but I think Jesse had threatened him if Virgil skipped out on him. Sonny Jenkins came around and talked to Virgil all afternoon. When he left he said he was taking out a warrant for Jesse's arrest, and that if he showed up again he'd be in jail so fast it'd make his head swim.

"So Virgil has been here all week. But he don't seem too happy. He stays mighty quiet, and he acts to me like he's looking over his shoulder every minute of the day."

Mother laid the letter on the table. Mattie picked it up and looked at Gran's careful handwriting on the lined page. She could see her grandmother bent over the kitchen table as she wrote. Virgil was probably off in one corner cleaning his gun, if he wasn't too afraid to go out to hunt.

There were lots worse things, she realized, than being cramped in this tiny house with an extra person.

"Mother," she said, "we've got to get Virgil away from there before something happens."

Mother and Daddy looked at her.

"You're probably right," Mother said. "If we go get him, it may be for keeps."

Mattie nodded.

"I thought he was a real thorn in your side," Daddy said.

"Well, he is . . . was, I guess. I don't know. It just doesn't seem right here anymore without him."

Mother reached over and squeezed her hand.

"I've got two days coming at the end of the week," Daddy said. "I'll drive up and get him. You can ride with me, Mattie."

Well, Mattie thought, having Virgil back ought to make my friends happy. Their cute Virgil will be here when school starts.

The thought of anyone pining for Virgil made her smile . . . until she remembered how lonesome she'd been the past two months.

The trip to Kentucky was pleasant. Mattie sat in the front seat with the window rolled down. When they reached the mountains, the air felt cool and fresh on her face. She fingered the cameo she'd fastened around her neck before she'd left. Mother wouldn't let her wear it except for special occasions. "It's all your grandmother will ever be able to give you, Mattie. We can't let anything happen to it," she told her.

When Mattie wore the cameo, she felt as if it were a bond drawing her to Gran. It made her forget the Gran who measured her against the work she could do and remember the Gran who was once a young bride with hopes and plans for the future. Gran was married at sixteen. Just three years older than I am now, Mattie thought. I wonder if in three years I'll think differently about boys, if I'll want to go to movies with them and dance with them.

She looked at Daddy. He was once a boy, she supposed, but he had turned out all right.

Then she laughed.

"What's so funny?" Daddy asked.

"Nothing. Everything. Daddy, when you were about thirteen, were you as awful as Virgil?"

"Worse. I drove everybody crazy, especially my

cousins, especially girls. Then I grew a little older and began to appreciate them." Now Daddy laughed. "I got to the point I much preferred the company of girls over the company of boys."

"Then you didn't mind when Janie Mae and I were both born girls?"

"Mind? What was to mind? You were healthy and beautiful."

Mattie nodded. At least he and Mother had their stories straight. But she couldn't let the subject drop.

"Did you ever wish you had a son?" Her voice shook slightly, and Daddy looked at her, the smile gone from his face.

"No, I never really wished for anything more than you two." He paused, then continued. "Except when I see pictures of children who need parents. Then I wish I could have them all for sons and daughters."

"Is that why you called Virgil 'son'?"

Daddy looked startled. "I didn't know I had done that. But I guess you're right. Virgil needs somebody." He gripped the steering wheel a little tighter. "And it doesn't look like Jesse is the right somebody."

Then he glanced again at Mattie. "But even if I had five hundred other children, that wouldn't make you and Janie Mae any less my own."

Mattie moaned. "And I bet all five hundred and four of us would have to live in that T.D.U."

She and Daddy laughed together, the sound first rippling from their throats, then threatening to shut off their breath.

They were still smiling as the car rolled down the mountain and into the mining camp.

When they stepped out in front of Gran's house,

Virgil came running around from the back yard.

"Gol-ol-lee," he said. "What're you doing here, Uncle Omer?"

"Mattie and I just decided to come out for an afternoon drive," Daddy said.

Virgil glanced at Mattie, then turned his attention back to Daddy. "Boy, Gran and Gramps will be surprised to see you. Can you stay a few days?"

"No, sorry, we have to head back tomorrow."

Mattie saw the disappointment in Virgil's face. And she knew it wasn't because he would be sorry to have only one day with her.

Daddy winked at her. "Reckon you can find room for us to sleep tonight?"

"Uncle Omer, you know Gran's always got room for you. But I wish you could stay awhile."

"We got to get on back. Lucy's planning to cook a special dinner for us tomorrow night. Sort of a celebration."

Virgil nodded. "Yeah, everybody's celebrating the end of the war. Aunt Mildred and Uncle Herbert can't stop grinning, they're so happy Jimmy Dale won't be fighting."

"We thought we'd celebrate something else, too."

Virgil looked at Daddy, his head cocked and the ever-present cowlick standing straight up.

"You tell him, Mattie," Daddy said.

"We thought you ought to come celebrate your birthday with us," she said.

"You mean . . ." Virgil's face broke into a broad smile. Mattie thought he looked like someone who'd seen the sun come up when he'd thought it wasn't anywhere near morning. "You mean you want me to go back with you?"

"That's just what we mean," Daddy said. "Reckon Gran and Gramps can spare you?"

"You bet! Gran! Gramps! Guess what!" Virgil shouted as he ran onto the porch.

Gran and Gramps came out the door. "Well, if it ain't one of my boys—nope, I mean my Mattie lass—come to see me," Gramps said, as he hurried down the steps and put his arm around Mattie.

Gran dabbed her eyes with the corner of her apron. "Well, this is a surprise," she said. "What brings you two to Kentucky?" Then she looked stricken. "Ain't nothing happened to Lucy or Janie Mae?"

Daddy reassured her that everyone was well.

Virgil puffed out his chest. "They've come to take me back with them," he said.

A smile broke over Mattie's face. "Yeah, the girls in Oak Ridge have been heartbroken long enough."

Virgil gave her a puzzled look.

"They're just waiting to see 'that cute Virgil' when school starts next week."

"Quit teasing me, Mattie."

"It's the truth, every word of it."

A flush crept up Virgil's neck, then spread onto his cheeks. Just as Mattie was thinking his hair was going to turn even redder than its usual hue, he burst out with a laugh.

"And I'll bet Robert is just waiting to see his 'cute Mattie.' "

Now Mattie felt the flush on her cheeks as Daddy and Gran and Gramps turned to look at her.

Virgil took one look at her face and sprinted around the house.

"I'll get you for that," she yelled as she ran after him.

She lowered her head and pushed her feet hard against the ground as she rounded the corner. She felt as if the earth were boosting her each time she lifted a foot, throwing her into the air the way a parent tosses a baby. The wind from her running blew the hair away from her face, and she wanted to laugh aloud.

But it was Virgil she heard laughing. "You'll never catch me," he called over his shoulder, "cause girls can't run as fast as boys."

Mattie put on a burst of speed. Talking and laughing had cost Virgil some momentum. He sprinted past the back gate, but Mattie was right behind him. She reached out a hand and lunged forward, catching the end of his shirt.

He looked around in surprise. Then, still laughing, he collapsed against the fence.

"I guess, Mattie McDowell," he said, gasping for air, "I guess some girls can run as fast as some boys."

"I guess,"—Mattie, too, was breathing hard—"I guess they can, Virgil Davis Turner McDowell."

Virgil stood straight and puffed out his chest. "Reckon I better go pack now."

He and Mattie went in the back door to the kitchen where Gran was busy putting plates on the table, ready to feed whoever came to her house.

AUTHOR'S NOTE

𝕏♪✻♪✻♪✻♪✻𝕏

IN THE EARLY 1940s THE UNITED STATES WAS
deeply involved in World War II. Efforts to win the war
occupied most of the population and the attention of
the public was so centered on war issues that other
concerns became secondary. When the atomic bomb
was dropped on Hiroshima, and then on Nagasaki, the
first reaction of most people was one of relief that the
war would be over. Reports on the extent of the dam-
age were slow to reach the public. Three days after the
explosion of the first bomb, there still were no esti-
mates of casualties and people celebrated victory.

The War At Home seeks to recreate this period in history. The author hopes that readers will understand the
celebration of the Oak Ridge residents as an expression
of joy that the secret project on which they had worked
played such an important part in ending the war. Their
tremendous rejoicing sprang from the hope that there
would be no more killing, not from a callous disregard
for the death and destruction caused by the atomic
bomb.